Darroch was pleased with the new Becky

Every time he praised the changes in the person he thought was Becky, Rebecca felt like a hypocrite. She mustn't overdo things. But she was discovering in herself the strongest, strangest urge to stand well in this man's eyes.

If it came to a showdown, if Becky failed to come back, if she herself failed to redeem this situation—would Darroch count it to her credit that at least she'd tried to keep them in comfort during the emergency at Craigievar?

Or would her thoughtless masquerade make him so furious he'd wipe the floor with her and send her packing?

Rebecca had no answers to these tormenting questions, only a scared, hollow feeling. She couldn't bear never to see Darroch again....

OTHER
Harlequin Romances
by ESSIE SUMMERS

Many of these titles are available at your local bookseller.

For a free catalogue listing all available Harlequin Romances,
send your name and address to:

HARLEQUIN READER SERVICE,
M.P.O. Box 707, Niagara Falls, N.Y. 14302
Canadian address: Stratford, Ontario, Canada N5A 6W2

One More River to Cross

by

ESSIE SUMMERS

Harlequin Books

TORONTO·LONDON·NEW YORK·AMSTERDAM
SYDNEY·HAMBURG·PARIS·STOCKHOLM

Original hardcover edition published in 1979
by Mills & Boon Limited

ISBN 0-373-02322-7

Harlequin edition published March 1980

This book is dedicated to our youngest grandchild,
Andrew David,
as requested by his sisters, Jennifer and
Kathryn Jack, the day after he was born.

———————◆———————

Printed in U.S.A.

CHAPTER ONE

REBECCA MENTEITH drove into Timaru, the sparkling waters of Caroline Bay to the east, the crooked line of Stafford Street running south before her, and westward downs and rolling hills that would, many miles on, lead her to the Southern Alps.

A month ago she'd thought that her new freelance career was to take her in a caravan she was picking up in Dunedin, to Fiordland first of all, where among the solitudes she was going to have a spirited attempt at writing a book instead of editing other people's efforts and news. But now, as had so often happened before, she must interrupt her plans and try, as Aunt Mirrie had said so despairingly, to sort her cousin out!

Still, this time it could have compensations. Her cousin appeared to be in the most adventurous spot possible, bang in the middle of mountains, remote, mysterious, challenging. A very odd place, surely, for that flibberty gibbet cousin of hers! But for once they'd thought that falling in love with a high-country farmer had wrought the seeming impossible.

Now Aunt Mirrie had the quaint idea that if her close cousin went to stay there, it wouldn't seem so frighteningly remote, so out of the world. 'She needs visitors, someone of her own, and you've always been able to brace her up, Rebecca. It's providential you're just off down south.'

Rebecca would have called it something else ... like a flaming nuisance. She'd planned and saved for two years to be able to leave the paper whose women's and children's page she edited, to hire a caravan from friends in Dunedin and keep herself for a year, while she endeavoured to write this novel that was just clamouring to

7

be written. Now she'd have to postpone making that
dream come true while she tried to get her cousin adjusted to living away back in the ranges after having
roved round the cities of the world a good deal of her
twenty-five years.

For a moment the first tinge of jealousy Rebecca had
ever known smote her. She herself had this inexplicable
longing to live among the mountains. Yet somehow she'd
never managed more than a day or two among them. She
hadn't learned to ski properly even, though her cousin,
travelling abroad so often with her parents, and visiting
some of the most sophisticated snow-sports areas of
Europe, was an expert on skis. That had been the one
thing that had made them all dare to hope that this new
engagement wasn't the disaster they feared.

You could see Cousin Becky amid all the glamour of
Swiss or French mountain resorts, amid the cafés and
hotels, gay and colourful, but not on a remote sheep-
station where sometimes an unbridged and flooded river
raged between the homestead and the access road.

It was strange that the two girls were so different,
especially in view of the fact that they could hardly be
told apart by their near and dear ones, and even shared
the same name. The likeness wasn't surprising. Their
mothers had been twin sisters, their fathers brothers.
They were often taken for identical twins. Rebecca was
an inch taller, a pound or two heavier. They both had the
same delicacy of features, an exquisite line of chin,
winged eyebrows, blue eyes, copper hair. But Rebecca
had a sturdiness of spirit that carried her impetuously
into all sorts of crusades and unorthodox adventures;
Becky was the clinging type.

Their mothers had laughed about the names. Becky
had been born in India where her father had held a post
for a couple of years. Rebecca had been born in New
Zealand. The two sisters, writing to each other in the
months of pregnancy, had exchanged ideas about names,

for boys and girls. Rebecca was to have been Prudence, which would have been a sad misnomer, and Becky Angela. Then at the time of the births, a week apart, with Rebecca the senior, each had been smitten with the idea the baby should be named for her maternal grandmother, and two Rebecca Menteiths were christened, thousands of miles apart.

But Alan Menteith's work in the diplomatic service had taken him into so many trouble spots of the world's surface, or into places where orthodox schooling was an impossibility, that the greater part of Becky's life had been spent in New Zealand with Rebecca's parents, with frequent and glamorous holidays with her own, who'd indulged her madly to make up for the time she'd had to spend away from them. In adult life it had been a great excuse for Becky not to have a regular job. That would have meant missing out on the holidays, the world travel, so she worked intermittently in her father's office, and even now, when he was back in New Zealand, relied mainly on his generous allowance.

Rebecca turned up a side-street in her rental car, found her hotel. She was going to stay the night before travelling west. Aunt Mirrie had booked it for her. 'I've told Becky that any time she feels the isolation is too much to bear, she's to go down to Timaru and stay there, booking it up to me. I do so want her to make a go of this. I'd like her settled at last.'

No wonder! This was Becky's third engagement, and Rebecca had a vague idea there had nearly been another. This last time Uncle Alan had tried to prevent it. No wonder, again! He'd said she'd soon tired of the others, but at least they'd both been suitable, whereas this was about the most incompatible set-up he'd ever heard of, for Becky. It wouldn't last five minutes, and she could stop planning a wedding and go down to see for herself what sort of a life these people lived. He had more than an idea it would be more than skiing and snow-sports!

Aunt Mirrie was scared that if Becky broke still another engagement, no man would take her on. What a mess! Becky had gone off vowing they'd see she had what it takes, that she believed Craigievar was one of the showplaces of the district, had been since pioneer days, and that Lennox's rich aunt, whose husband had farmed it many years ago, was willing to put money in to acquire a large piece of land for him ... they reckoned land in thousands of acres there, not hundreds ... build them a lovely new house, and when this was done, the estate would have access to new and exciting ski-fields that had recently been opened up, and when a bridge to Heronscrag, an adjoining estate, was finished, they would no longer be cut off by a temperamental river. So they'd had hopes.

But now, according to Becky's letters home—her parents now lived in Auckland and so did Rebecca—the family were treating her shockingly. All this made Rebecca most unsure that they would welcome as a visitor a girl who looked an absolute replica of the one they resented. If they'd taken a scunner at Becky, they wouldn't want two of her! However, she was coming south, and it seemed selfish to refuse Aunt Mirrie and not even to see at first hand how things were. She'd ring Becky from here, suggest she come to Timaru for a few days' break, then travel back with her.

She parked her car, went to the reception desk. 'I've a room booked for a day or two. Rebecca Menteith is the name.'

The receptionist boggled at her. 'But—but you came and got your key not a quarter of an hour ago.' She gazed, fascinated, at the case Rebecca had put down. '*And* you took your case up then. I—I'm sorry, but I just don't get this.'

Rebecca too looked blank. 'I've just this moment arrived from Christchurch. I think there's been some mistake. I—oh, I know.' She grinned. 'That would be my cousin, same name, same looks and just a week younger than I. We've got mixed up all our lives. She's living up beyond Lake Tekapo, and I'm going up to stay with her. She must have decided to come down to meet me, and it was her mother who booked my room for me. Sorry to get you so confused. I suppose she thought she might as well rest in my room.'

The woman said slowly, 'I wish she'd explained. You could have been upset we've given someone else your key.'

Rebecca smiled sympathetically. 'I know. It wouldn't occur in that light to Becky. She'd have something else on her mind and decide it was easier this way. I do apologise for her.'

The woman swallowed, still gazing. 'I thought I was seeing things when you asked for your key. It was like a replay on television. You said cousins, not identical twins. I've never seen twins more alike.'

'Our mothers *were* identical twins, our fathers brothers, though not twins. So we're double cousins. A freak happening of the same genes being reproduced, I suppose. I've got a brother, but nothing less like me could be imagined. He's as black as the ace of spades. But being so like each other—Becky and me—has caused a lot of trouble at times. I'll go up and see her now.'

The receptionist said, 'She didn't look very well. Perhaps that was why she thought she'd like to settle in to wait for you. By the way, it happens to be a twin room as we didn't have a single vacant, so if she wants to stay, no problem.'

'I think she might easily want to, so thank you very much. What number?' With that she was on her way, a sinking feeling at her heart. If it was evident to a stranger that Becky wasn't exactly blooming, then she could be in for a trying time. She loved Becky, without really admiring her, but——

She tapped at the door, went in. Becky was sitting in a

basket chair looking out of the window, her very attitude listless and dejected. When she realised it was her cousin she sprang up, rushed at her, flung her arms about her. 'Oh, Rebecca, I didn't dream you'd be here before lunch. I'm so glad you are! I couldn't stand that horrible place and people a moment longer, so I ran away.' She burst into tears.

She'd have to have her cry out, Rebecca knew, so she uttered soothing sounds, patted her back. She took herself to task; she mustn't be too unsympathetic. Becky might, this time, have been through a very trying experience. It would be too horrible for anyone to visit future in-laws and find she wasn't welcome, especially in such isolation.

It was some time before Becky was coherent. 'Perhaps I ought to have known what it would be like,' she managed at last, 'but when Lennox told me about it I thought it sounded just like a continuation of the sort of life at the Chateau ... all skiing and fabulous meals and a sort of Swiss touch.'

Rebecca hid a smile, but said, 'And instead you found it was life lived in quite primitive conditions. That was only to be expected, love. You and Lennox met on Ruapehu in an artificial atmosphere, you fell in love with the surroundings there, and Lennox himself, you came up to Auckland with him, had all the excitement of the engagement, then after only a very short time of exchanging love-letters, you came on down here to a high-country sheep-station.

'It sounds glam, but it is after all just a glorified and very isolated farm, where even if they do go round the sheep on skis in the depths of winter, it's mainly, I imagine, ordinary farm routine, only in extra harsh, tough conditions. But it does give you near access to a new ski-field. There would be compensations. And Lennox is the sort of guy to give any girl a quickened pulse.'

Becky sighed. 'Easy to be philosophical, Rebecca,

when you haven't got to endure it yourself. How would you like to be cut off from all your newspaper contacts, the interesting people you meet, the city doings?'

Rebecca said gently, 'But Becky, that's just what I'm doing, isn't it? Getting a caravan and hieing off to the solitudes to write a book.'

'It won't last. You'll pine for people.'

'I could. But then I wouldn't have a husband with me.'

'Trouble was, Lennox wasn't there half the time. The men would be working outside, sometimes up at the huts for days at a time, while I was cooped up from morning till night, snowed under with the most awful household chores—not a hope of getting any help in. And outside everything so bare, stark and grim. Life's quite crude at times, not just tough.'

'What about Mrs Ewan Fordyce? Wouldn't she cope with most of it and just expect you to lend a hand? Your letters to me didn't say much. Is she——'

'She wasn't too bad, but has to spend so long in the schoolroom with the children's lessons—they're on correspondence school. In my opinion—and I told them so —they'd be far better at boarding-school, even if they are small, and they expected me to run the house to leave Sylvie more time at it. At least Darroch Fordyce did. He told me straight what he expected.'

'Who's he?' asked Rebecca. 'I had very little time with Lennox when he was in Auckland, but I remember him mentioning only Ewan.'

'He's Ewan's brother. Very dour. Younger than Ewan but seems to own Craigievar which used to be their aunt's property. But I think Darroch went up there first. Their own father is in shipbuilding in Port Chalmers— I think the aunt must be on the father's side. She's rolling in money—still has shares in the property.

'Ewan and Sylvie have a lovely new and convenient house on the estate, but with Ewan in South America buying cattle—or perhaps he's selling cattle—she came down to the old homestead. Ewan didn't like her on her own. It's not fair, you know, this South American trip was brought forward. Lennox was to have gone later, I thought we'd have been married then and I could have gone with him. Now Mother and Dad are settled permanently in New Zealand I miss the travel I'm used to.'

Rebecca forbore to say that most girls these days made it under their own steam, went on working holidays round the world.

Becky continued: 'It wouldn't have been so bad if they'd not been stupid enough to let their housekeeper go off to Australia for a long holiday to see her married daughter, because I was coming. Ever hear anything like that? I think Lennox was stringing me on a bit ... and so I've told him ... made out they were wealthier than they are. What's the use of saying they're worth so much, when it's all tied up in thousands of acres of barren mountains? What sort of a holiday was that for me? Really, Rebecca, no shops, no other people, only everlasting stupid sheep and keas crying and avalanches roaring and the ground so hard—in September!—that you could actually hear those ridiculous cats walking on it!'

Rebecca blinked. '*Ridiculous* cats? How can cats be ridiculous?' (She must try to get Becky to see the funny side of something.)

Becky said scathingly, 'Their names! An enormous ginger one, always shedding its hair, called Mehitabel, a black and white tomcat that leapt about like a springer spaniel, called Jumping Jehosaphat, and a tortoiseshell one called Zachariah. Rebecca, I know you love cats, but I was trying to tell you all that went on up there. You've got to help me. I'm in an awful position!' She gulped, shuddered. 'They have the vastest quantities of food, even now, and all they talked about to me, if they weren't talking sheep and being snowbound or floodbound, was of the old days when the stores came in once a year when they backloaded. That means when they came in, across the river in wagons, to take the wool bales out, they brought in the year's supply of sugar, flour, and so on. Any woman who went up there under those conditions must have been raving mad! Lamps and fires in every room to stop the water-pipes freezing in winter ... and they speak of it *romantically*!'

She paused to say, 'Don't look like that ... all interested. That's just your journalistic mind. I can just see you writing it up, but believe me, it's a different kettle of fish enduring a life like that. When I objected to some of the bullocking work I was expected to do and said it wasn't much of a holiday, that Darroch said it wasn't meant to be a holiday, that he'd told Lennox to get me down here without delay so I knew what living in the high-country entailed. Anybody'd think he was Lennox's father instead of his cousin,' she grumbled. 'He said I needed to take off my rose-coloured spectacles and confront the reality of the back of beyond ... if I really meant to marry Lennox, if it wasn't just the infatuation that sprang up on a snow-sports holiday.

'I asked what the diamonds on my finger meant if not just that, and he said well, he'd always thought of engagements as a trial run before marriage and that in the high-country it was always considered wise to get prospective brides to try it out before the knot was tied, and if I couldn't take it, now was the time to say so.'

It did sound stark, almost brutal ... surely this Darroch Fordyce could have handled it more gently. It sounded as if he wanted the engagement to be broken. The life up there probably hardened men and they couldn't realise what a shock it would be to anyone like Becky. Her father had been in trade missions and diplomatic posts most of his life, and Becky's life, when she'd not been back in New Zealand at school with Rebecca, had been one of dinner-parties, receptions, cocktail evenings, travel. London, Paris, Munich, Toronto ... and now a high-country sheep-station, hemmed in by the Main Divide of the Southern Alps, with an unbridged river as the other boundary. Honesty made Rebecca recognise that Darroch Fordyce had the right of it. But he sounded extremely autocratic.

Becky was sweeping on. 'Then I found Lennox didn't have as much as a share in it. Darroch said he was still winning his spurs, that when this aunt felt he had what it takes for there, she might buy him in some property. She sounds a real dragon. Comes up from time to time, but not while I was there, thank goodness. She was in England—might even be on her way back by now. Rolling in money . . . trips round the world while other people slave to bring in the cash for her to do it. She still has a financial interest in the estate.'

Rebecca said crisply, 'Was she one of the women of the earlier days who put up with no conveniences?'

Becky looked sulky, said reluctantly, 'Well, yes. But believe me, she's got it made now. Her husband died long ago and she's had it easy for a long time.'

'Did she leave there when her husband died?'

'No. She ran it with her son for some time, but his health broke down. No wonder! He needs to be near city hospitals. So her nephews run it. It's given her a sort of complex. She holds the moneybags, is willing to buy in more land for Lennox and build him a house—if she's got money like that he ought to persuade her to buy him a farm near Timaru. Easier access to markets and transport, I told him. I said it would be in his best interests, that that was why I wanted it instead of seeing him kill himself up there.'

'How did Lennox feel about that?' asked Rebecca.

Becky looked astonished, remembering. 'He wouldn't even consider it, Rebecca. Said I'd get used to the mountains, that women did.' She spread her hands out in a despairing gesture. 'And I couldn't move him from that position. So I quit.'

Rebecca was trying to take it in. 'Quit? But you're still wearing his ring.'

Becky subdued a sob. 'I had enough sense not to burn my bridges. Lennox worships the ground I walk on. He'll come to it.'

Rebecca felt disturbed. She hated that phrase ... 'worships the ground I walk on!' What a state of affairs that must be! Quite unreal, not a modern outlook. Marriage was a partnership, not goddess worship. It was odd. Becky was a weak character who always dropped her bundle when the going got hard, but there was a tenacious streak in her that was very hard to cope with and if Lennox was indeed besotted, he just might leave the life he loved and settle for an existence that would never satisfy him.

Rebecca had liked and respected him when she'd met him, but there'd been no time to really size him up. She said firmly, 'Then how *did* you quit?'

Becky looked a little evasive. Rebecca's heart sank recognising the signs. Becky would tell some of the truth, but not the whole truth, probably. 'Well, the men were up one of the valleys moving sheep. Sylvie was busy in the schoolroom. A huge truck came in over the river with a terrific load of drums. Sylvie asked me to see to his morning tea—the driver's. I'd known the day before he was coming and hoped I might get out with him. I had my case packed and my note written. I just knew I'd have to take drastic action to get them to understand how much it means to me to live within reach of town. Everyone thinks I'm incapable of making decisions, so they badger me ... even you do, Rebecca, and Dad. But this time I did it on my own and I reckon I'll have convinced Lennox this is the only way.

'I said I was going home, that this was to test Lennox's love for me. It was a very good letter. I said I had no intention of spending the rest of my life on a barren spit of land at the headwaters of a river in the Southern

Alps. That if Lennox wanted me he'd have to settle for a place within ten miles of town! What do you think of that?'

Rebecca drew in a deep breath. 'What do I think? I think you've probably blotted your copybook and lost Lennox.'

An hour later they were still talking and Becky, intent on Rebecca seeing the situation for herself, was wearing down her resistance. Becky said desperately, 'You can't possibly lecture me like this, when you haven't seen the terrain. You've never been up against conditions like this. These mountains aren't like Ruapehu which is a winter playground. These are harsh and pitiless mountains and men are mad to have sheep-runs there and expect wives to face the life. You'll change your mind when you see them.

'That family up there must know the say-so isn't all theirs, that I have the backing of my family just as Lennox has the backing of his. You might easily persuade him it would be better for all of us living nearer civilisation. They said themselves they've got to live amicably together. You've got to see it, Rebecca.'

That could be true. She must be able to report to Aunt Mirrie, because as sure as God made little apples, another broken engagement was in the offing. Better than a broken marriage, certainly, but with Becky's last few years littered with such ruptures, her poor mother and father had done more than their fair share of explaining and excusing to their circle of friends. Could this breach be healed?

Becky saw the indecision on her cousin's face and pressed on. 'I think they'd respect you for going up there. They're very family-minded. They just think of me as a ... as a sort of bird of paradise ... you know, gorgeous but just flitting through their drab lives and not to be taken seriously.'

Rebecca hid a smile. Becky plunged on, 'But they

ought to know *I* have a solid, respectable family behind me too. They just think my parents have no roots, lead a very cosmopolitan existence. People on the land are like that.'

Rebecca said doubtfully, 'Most farming folk have a very good grip of the political situation—their markets are world markets and people like your father have to negotiate such things. I hardly think they'd feel that. But you're overwrought, Becky, and can't see it in quite the right perspective.'

'Then in fairness you've got to get up there and see it for yourself. Don't let me down now, Rebecca, you never have before.'

When she capitulated, Becky embraced her. 'You're so good with interviews, being in newspaper work ... I'm confident you can make them see my side of it. I knew if I could get to you, you'd make a difference. Make them see I'm quite willing to marry a *down*-country farmer.'

Well, she was committed now. 'I don't want them to have warning I'm coming up. They may be so furious with you walking out on them and just leaving a note, they may not want to have any other Menteith there. I'll just arrive. Is this river likely to be fordable most of the time? I can just turn up and get across?'

'Oh, yes. It's nothing like the Pawerawera at Dragonshill. Before they got their bridge it was terribly dangerous, always quicksands after flood. The Whakarite isn't like that. Take it gently. It's got a good shingle bed.'

Rebecca knew she was a fool. It would be anything but pleasant, but there was probably truth in what Becky said, that it might help to have a close relative on Becky's side turning up to discuss the situation. And if she could spare Aunt Mirrie any anxiety, she would. She had just nursed Uncle Alan through an illness that had been very dangerous and was in no shape to travel down here.

She put through a call to her Dunedin friends to say

she'd not be picking up her caravan for a few days yet as she was diverting to Lake Tekapo way to visit her cousin and would let them know later when to expect her.

Becky decided to stay in Timaru till Rebecca could report how things were at Craigievar. 'Lennox will have cooled off by now, I think, and if you tell him I've stayed here instead of going right up to Auckland, he could be thrilled not to have to chase me that far. He could come down, and we could look around properties in this area.'

Rebecca felt she couldn't be blunt and tell her not to count on it. What if Lennox realised that it was just no use? That Becky would never settle on any farm, distant or far?

She said, 'Becky, can you lend me some thick sweaters? Well, a couple. I'd intended to shop for some of those gorgeous natural wool ones you can get down South, so I'm not very well equipped for an Alpine adventure.'

Becky was only too glad. She'd brought most of her stuff, she explained, to make them realise she was serious about not being able to stay up there. She seemed to be feverishly anxious to get Rebecca on her way, so Rebecca thought she must really care for Lennox more than she had for the previous men in her life. Rebecca shut out the inner voice that was telling her what a fool she was to allow herself to become involved in what could be a sticky situation with this dour family who appeared to be trying to break up her cousin's engagement. Oh, well, she'd been involved in Becky's affairs all her life and usually came off without any lasting damage. So be it.

Ninety-five miles to Tekapo, then about twenty miles travelling right to the edge of the Southern Alps, the range that ran like a mighty backbone on the far side of the South Island of New Zealand. They were lovely miles if only she hadn't been filled with apprehension about her reception at Craigievar. She knew she must keep an open mind about these people. Becky was given to instant likes and dislikes. All Becky seemed to want her to do was to confirm to her father that these people were impossible, that they were crude, intolerant, hidebound.

She formulated half a dozen gambits for the moment of meeting, only to spurn them all in turn. She could say: 'As you can see, I'm Becky's cousin.' (This was if Lennox didn't come to the door because he just might have set off after Becky already.) Then she could say, 'I hope you don't find this an intrusion, but my aunt was very anxious, and I wondered if I just might be able to help.'

Perhaps it would be better to begin, 'You'll be surprised to see me ... Becky's cousin ... when she's not here, but we met in Timaru and I wondered if we could have a little chat about things.' How feeble! No, she'd just have to act as the occasion seemed to demand. They might be surly, reticent people who would resent her. Yet surely, seeing they'd thought Lennox's fiancée should come to look over the terrain, was it so surprising that Becky's mother, unable to travel because her husband's diet still demanded close attention, had asked her niece to call? Ah, that would be the line to take, if she could get it out in that awkward moment of arrival. And if they resented her too obviously, then she wouldn't stay with them, but would go back to Tekapo township.

That gave her pause for thought. It was developing into wild tussocky country once she was over the downs and through the mountain passes. And she had a river crossing to face. What if they got into a lengthy discussion and then she felt she could not trespass on their hospitality? She wouldn't care to encounter engine or tire trouble on roads like these, with perhaps twenty or so miles between homesteads. She would stay in Tekapo overnight.

She was glad next morning she had done just that. The next lap of her journey was over a road that hardly justified the name, even though the background to it was singularly beautiful.

At first it ran by Lake Tekapo. Rebecca had visited the Southern Lakes before, with friends, and had marvelled at their blueness, that varied from sapphire to azure, from cornflower to cobalt, according to the day, even if it was basically due to their being snow-fed waters. But this was turquoise, opaque, milky, with streaks of green here and there, shimmering like an opal, with, on the far rim, mountains of a faery-like quality such as one might see in a dream-world.

Among the tussock now were the larger, coarser tufts of snow-grass, stony slopes, barren stretches of shingle and boulders, and the road was deeply rutted after the recent thaw from a winter of frozen-hard tracks. What a horizon now ... bounded wholly by mountains. Her arms were tired with the effort of holding the steering-wheel so that she stayed in the most comfortable of the ruts, if any could be called that, so as one rut flattened out she drew into the side and took out a flask of coffee.

A small lake lay to her right, a signpost declaring it was called Moana Waitatoa. As a journalist she never travelled without a Maori dictionary. She flicked over the pages. Moana was lake, of course, and Wai water, but what was Totoa? It meant stormy. Lake of Stormy Waters! Well, she knew she was heading for stormy waters, but did even the scenery have to remind her of that?

She munched a biscuit, studied her map. The homestead was marked on the foot of a huge range, across the Whakarite. She thumbed the dictionary again. Whaka, a prefix giving to an adjective or verb the sense of 'the act of' ... act of what, in this case? The next moment she was laughing. The act of decision, if she was interpreting it rightly, because like so many words in Maori, with an alphabet of only fifteen letters, it could have several meanings. There was a star beside the name of the river . . . she looked for the asterisk below . . . here was the English rendering: The Rubicon. To take an irrevocable step! So it might prove for her. Oh, how foolish! It would be Becky who would take that irrevocable step if she married into this family. But what was ahead of Rebecca? Victory or defeat? Would she be able to ameliorate the position, or aggravate it? Only time would tell.

The road became a track, the track began to dwindle, till at last it came to a stop beside a shallow, shingle-bedded river bed that didn't look half as fearsome as so many New Zealand river beds. Possibly in its lower reaches as it would spread out over plain and downland, to become the braided river-course that was the normal, with countless streams intersected by great reefs of shingle, except in times of flood, but here, so soon after it emerged from the mountains, it was all one stream, and at present, with the great snows still frozen in the clefts of the mountains, it purled along quite gently.

Praise the saints it was low. If she was sent packing with her tail between her legs, it would be easy enough to ford again. There was a garage of sorts on the bank, with an open front and room for several vehicles. There was a good car there, kept for times when the river was too high for a smart vehicle, she guessed, an ancient farm truck, even a waggon, kept in good repair. She went in. There was a phone on the bench with instructions for anyone to call the homestead to give the handle three turns. Well, not for her . . . she was going in unheralded.

She got back in the car, slid down the bank very carefully, in her lowest gear, felt very firm bottom, ground slowly through. There hadn't been rain for days. This

was just like some of the shallow streams up north she'd
forded on picnic days.

She grinned to herself as she came up the other
bank ... she had crossed her Rubicon! Now for the
house to face Darroch and Lennox and Sylvie Fordyce.
Of them all she feared this Darroch most. She had met
and liked Lennox.

The house was on an elevation, well out of reach of
flood water, she guessed. Only larches and Douglas firs
grew around the lower reaches, and then they were well
back from the twisting drive. Too much shade would
make for icy conditions. In winter the sun would go
down behind the ranges of the Great Divide before three.
She admitted it was more fearsome than she'd imagined,
but also more magnificent. There was a breadth and a
sweep and height upon height that spelt vision and challenge.

She came up into a garden that was almost lifeless
under the onslaughts of winter just past, but in the
straggly bushes and withered plants you could see sum-
mertime must have decked it with colour, and even now
a rock garden that covered an entire slope held splashes
of lime, sulphur, rust-red, silver-grey, in the lichens and
alpine ground plants that patched it.

Her heart thudded against her side as she stepped out,
and at the very moment a door in the middle of a long
glassed-in porch opened and out stepped a rugged giant
of a man with massive shoulders, a face as craggy as the
mountain behind him, dressed in rough shepherding
clothes ... and even his colouring seemed a blend of the
tussock and shingle colours of the terrain that was his
habitat and his livelihood.

Astonishment was written all over him. He waited for
her to climb the steps to him. As she reached the top her
voice failed her.

But he spoke first. 'I can't believe it,' he said. 'I just
can't believe it! Tell me, is this a return, penitent and

hopeful, or is it just that you've forgotten something? Is is possible you've heard of the hole we're in and by some extraordinary attack of conscience, you've come to see if any help is better than none? Is it, Becky, because if it is, for Lennox's sake, I'll let you stay to try to prove yourself! And perhaps by the time he gets back from Auckland you'll know your own mind! He's flown there after you. Did you get no further than Tekapo? Did you hear from the grapevine there?'

Her wits deserted her. 'Hear what?' she asked.

'That Sylvie is being rushed to hospital—oh, not in danger, but fairly acute. The doctor took her straight in—gallstones. This isn't our week, is it? Lennox haring after you to Auckland, Ewan in South America ... and three children here to be looked after and all my men up at the huts! But at least *you're* back ... better than nothing!'

Rebecca gulped. He sounded as if, in these circumstances, he'd give Becky another chance. Oh, if only she'd persuaded Becky to come back with her! This was a chance in a million ... and she'd muffed it. If only she'd insisted Becky come back to face the music. To talk things out instead of leaving a runaway's note! Instead of trying to play God herself, she ought to have made Becky see she could only work out a solution at Craigievar itself.

With that instinctive clamouring for help all souls know in emergencies, she found herself muttering inwardly, 'Show me what to do, God, show me what to do.' Afterwards she was to jeer at herself to think she'd kidded herself she was praying ... because did one ever pray for help to deceive? Or should one? Well, she didn't know, but her response was automatic, almost jerked out of her ... in a voice that even to her own ears sounded more like Becky's than her own, she said, 'I was disgusted with myself for giving up so quickly, Darroch. I don't expect you to understand ... but it was all so

different from what I'd imagined. I'll give it another go.'
In that moment, brief as it was, she knew what she was
going to do ... take Becky's place for a couple of days
and somehow get her cousin up here, unknown to the
others, and swap places. This was Becky's one chance to
prove herself and save her engagement.

Darroch Fordyce still looked as if he couldn't believe
it and just stood staring. Then he looked at the car and
demanded, 'Where did you get that?'

She dared not tell the truth and say Christchurch.
Becky wouldn't have had time to get that far and back.
She hoped there was nothing in the registration numbers
to give it away, and said, 'Timaru. It's a rental.'

'Oh ... good idea. You'll return it to Fairlie, I suppose.'

'Yes.' She was grateful for that much acceptance.
'Now, don't worry too much, Darroch. We'll manage
somehow.'

He wasn't to know that wasn't Becky speaking, but
Rebecca. She was sure if he knew she was Becky's
cousin, up here to look the lie of the land over, he'd pack
her off, and some woman was needed to help this household right now. She was committed ... had crossed her
Rubicon in more ways than one!

CHAPTER TWO

REBECCA had to keep going; she dared not give herself time to think. She said weakly, 'Where are the children at the moment? Are they very upset, poor lambs?' He looked surprised. She'd have to watch her step. Becky wasn't given to calling children poor lambs. She'd probably been even a little hostile towards them. That Rebecca couldn't be, but she mustn't over-fuss.

He said, 'I've given them some outside chores to do, clearing out the nest-boxes and putting fresh straw in and so on. Well, I'll take your things to your room again. By the way, the kids don't know you cleared out. Sylvie just told them you'd gone to Fairlie for a few days. They think Len's off to a sheep sale. We thought they'd pester him with questions otherwise, when he returns. Normally we'd not deceive them, but you put us in a very awkward position.'

She sounded contrite. 'I know. I must have had a brainstorm. It—it was all so different from what I've been used to. It got on top of me suddenly. Oh, when do you think Lennox will be back?'

(She had to know so she could make plans to get Becky back here by talking sense to her over the phone. She'd really come into disfavour in the district if she didn't appear to pull her weight in this emergency.)

'I've no idea. He said he'd ring me when he caught up with you. You'd better ring your parents tonight, tell them you ran away but came back, and if Len turns up tell him to come back here. Last night, I was so flaming mad with you I'd have packed you straight off again, thinking a clean cut was the better, but right now I can feel I'm mellowing a bit. Only a bit, mind you, because I daresay it took guts to come back. And, surprisingly,

27

you seem ready to help out. What's the reason behind that? Is it true what everyone says, that there's no room for two women in one kitchen? That you'd like to give it a go on your own?'

'Something like that. Oh, that sounds awful. I'm terribly sorry about Sylvie, but it could be I'll be better on my own.'

'That being so,' said Darroch Fordyce, 'when Sylvie comes back, Ewan should be home and they'll go over to their place, of course. They can take the shepherds for meals, and you can have a shot at cooking just for Lennox and me. How's that?'

Rebecca swallowed. She was trying to tread a middle course, not to appear too much changed too suddenly, yet more eager to pitch in than Becky had been. She managed, 'Sounds a good thing, but maybe I ought to try more than that. Sylvie couldn't cook for extra men when convalescent, so you'd better let them eat here just the same.'

A gleam of what might have been faint respect dawned in the light tussocky-brown eyes under that thatch of bleached hair. Then she realised with dismay that if she did get Becky back, her cousin would be furious at having to tackle cooking for five! Well, she'd just have to play it along.

'At the moment, Becky, they're up at No. Two Hut blissfully unaware of both your departure and Sylvie's. They won't be down till tomorrow, so they can think what the kids thought, that Lennox is off to Timaru to the sale. Come on in ... I'll be glad to turn dinner and kids over to you because after we've had a snack lunch I ought to go up the Bluff Block and move some sheep.' He paused, added, 'Don't go off the deep end, but in the next few days you've got a fine chance to show us you are, after all, made of the stuff high-country wives should be. If so I'll withdraw my objections to the match.'

Rebecca almost choked. Very autocratic! He was only

Lennox's cousin, when all was said and done, and just a few years his senior. No wonder Becky hadn't found it easy. She ought to have fought back. Rebecca would have done.

She waved him on with the case, avoiding another pitfall. She'd be supposed to know her own room. It was a pleasant surprise. She'd expected to find it extremely sparsely furnished, with a plaid rug on the bed, utility furniture. The bed had colonial spool ends, the dressing-table was surely an antique, with a mirror stand upon it. The bedspread was white cotton knitted, over a turquoise frilled valance. The curtains were sheer white terylene billowing out in the cool mountain breeze and framed by chintzy drapes in soft lavender and turquoise. She bit back an exclamation of pleasure. Watch it, Rebecca!

He dropped the case on the floor, said, 'You know where to wash up and so on. I'll rustle up a chop and fried-up potatoes. And I'll ring the gong for the kids. I daresay they might be glad you're back.'

'*Might*,' said Rebecca, grinning. 'On the principle of any port in a storm?'

He turned, surprised, one brow lifted. 'Much, much better! I thought Lennox had got himself a wench without a sense of humour. Were you just too scared of us to let yourself go? If so, sorry.'

'Something like that,' she said thankfully. If he was going to make excuses for her supposedly former behaviour, it might make things easier. Now there was the hurdle of the children. There were two boys, one girl— Robert, Andrew, Nan. She must look for some indication as to which was Robert, which Andrew.

The bathroom, toilet and shower doors all had fancy labels on them, praise be. She could hear Darroch Fordyce busy at the stove so walked confidently in that direction. She came into an enormous kitchen with a double-oven diesel-fed fuel stove in blue and cream roaring away. Cooking oil was heating and some delicious-looking middle-loin chops were sizzling and in another frying-pan, with some expertise, Darroch Fordyce was arranging thick slices of left-over potato. Thankfully she saw a loaf on a board and began to slice into it, took a chance that the cupboard near the fridge was the every-day one, opened it and found jam, butter, honey, even some cake-tins. She pulled open the wrong drawer for cutlery, muttered, 'What am I doing?' as anyone might, and pulled open the next to find all she sought.

Voices off, and Darroch looked out, said, 'Heaven help us, they're letting young Andrew carry the eggs! He's far too young.' So Rebecca was able to identify the boys.

They came helter-skelter along the back porch, and Darroch hastily grabbed the eggs. 'I know it's tempting when the others run, Andrew, but the one who carries the eggs walks. Yes, I know you didn't crash, but you might next time. What did you say, Rob? Whose car? It's a rental. Becky went as far as Timaru with the truck-driver, and decided to hire a car to drive back. Where've you got to leave it, Becky? Oh, you said Fairlie, didn't you? You'd better go down with it tomorrow or the next day. It'll cost you the earth otherwise. Fortunately the river's low. Any chance of it rising and I'll take it across to the bank for you.'

She hoped there'd be no rising. It would suit her very well to get down to Fairlie soon, if she could get Becky to meet her there and return here, taking Rebecca's place and endeavouring to prove herself capable in a family crisis.

The children weren't enthusiastic about her return, but not antagonistic either. Andrew, who was only four, asked hopefully, 'When's Mummy coming home? To-night?'

Robert was scornful. 'Silly ... you can't just whip scores of gallstones out of a person and let them come back right away. It's not like having a tooth out. She'll be away ages.'

Darroch said quickly, 'But we'll go down to Timaru to see her in hospital, so that'll be fun. We'll get you some more Lego when we're in town, and that train too.'

A good diversion. In strolled a large cat with a splendid marmalade coat. It weaved across the room, rubbed itself against Rebecca's legs. Nan said, 'Goodness, she's never done that before.' Rebecca bent down, scratched between its ears, said, 'Good afternoon, Mehitabel ... you're a fabulous beastie except for shedding your hairs ... but with these trews, it doesn't matter.' Mehitabel responded with an outsized purr, turned on her back, waving her paws in mid-air inviting a tummy-rub. 'Good heavens,' said Darroch Fordyce, 'you're even getting used to our felines now.'

Another hurdle taken. But this impersonation business had more to it than met the eye. She could see pitfalls yawning before her feet every moment of every day that lay ahead. God grant there weren't many of them!

Fortunately there wasn't time to stop, to think, to panic. That, no doubt, would descend upon her when she went to bed that night. At present she must concentrate on appearing familiar with the set-up every single moment.

She'd cooked on a coal range on a camping trip once, and used both gas and electric stoves in her time, but had never even seen a diesel-operated fuel stove before. Possibly it never needed stoking, only blazing up, but she had no know-how at all. Would Becky, that lily-of-the-field, have been forced into helping with the meals here or would it be safe to ask to be shown? She decided not to risk it but was saved anyway when before Darroch Fordyce went outside he said with a slightly scornful inflection, 'Now you've been pitchforked into being housekeeper, I'd better be magnanimous and instead of saying don't you wish you'd taken an interest in the stove before, show you how it works. Actually, it's on day and night and is drip-fed, so less trouble than a coal-stove, believe me. Of course in summer we use the electric range out in the small work-kitchen, but this supplies us with never-failing hot water, and has such a huge top, you can always sizzle or simmer, braise or bake ... the lot.' He began to demonstrate.

Rebecca expressed heartfelt thanks. He looked at her sharply. Oh dear, she mustn't overdo it. She said, 'Anyway, I'm sure Nan will keep me right if I make any blueys.'

Nan, who was as red-haired as Rebecca, said, 'What's a bluey?' Rebecca said carelessly, 'It's our usual term for mistakes in the journalistic world.'

Darroch Fordyce raised one of the penthouse eyebrows. 'Have you had experience in that ... journalism?'

'Oh, only in a superficial way. Some of Dad's reports had to be printed and he usually roped me in for proofreading and what-have-you, so I picked up the jargon.'

'I noticed you'd a portable typewriter in the car. Hadn't noticed you had one with you when you first came up.'

She said quickly, 'I must have had it in one of my cases. You know how it is ... you never have enough hands or fingers, so the more things in your cases the better.'

He nodded, 'And with your people travelling so much, you'd know all the wrinkles.'

Rebecca tucked that reminder away. She hoped Darroch hadn't travelled much himself. If he had, and he and Becky had already discussed places they'd both visited, he might refer to them again and she'd fall flat on her face.

'I'll be fairly handy. Bang the gong if you need me. The youngsters can come with me till afternoon-tea time. That'll keep them out of your hair.'

She was relieved. That meant she could explore, so

that she'd appear as familiar with the house as Becky would be. Also she could get that phoning done with no one within earshot. Imagine if Darroch had stood over her, practically, while she rang Auckland, presumably trying to contact Lennox. Just think if he'd reached Becky's home by now, and she had to pretend to him, because Darroch was there, that she was Becky. It didn't bear thinking about.

First she'd ring the Timaru Hotel, make Becky realise she had a chance in a thousand of redeeming herself, and get her to beat it back to Fairlie as soon as possible, where they could switch identities. As soon as she saw four backs disappear, she got going. Darroch might expect a toll-call to Auckland on his bill, but not a Timaru one, so without a qualm she booked it to her father's number in Hamilton. Poor Dad!

She felt relief. If she was lucky, in a moment she'd hear her cousin's voice and insist she come back here to take her place. She must then circumvent any idea Darroch might have of following her to Fairlie to bring her back when she'd returned the rental car. If she went there alone, she could then get Becky to take the bus to Tekapo, and arrange for Darroch to meet the bus, and if they changed clothes in Fairlie, he'd never guess it wasn't the same girl who'd driven off earlier in the day.

She got the receptionist and immediately her heart was in her boots as she heard: 'Sorry, Miss Menteith, your cousin checked out two hours ago, I think she was taking the express to Christchurch. Does that help you? Will you know where to contact her there?'

Rebecca managed to utter thanks, hang up. Then she felt limp. Becky was the utter limit! She'd promised to wait in Timaru till Rebecca could report on things up here. This was the last time, positively the last, she'd ever try to help her! How dared Becky enlist her aid and then disappear into thin air! What now? Only one thing to do ... ring Aunt Mirrie and report. And confess she'd made things worse by embarking on a mad masquerade. Even if she'd acted from the best of motives, playing for time and trying to save the situation, she'd really bungled things. Aunt Mirrie came on the line.

Rebecca begged her to hear her out. She finished up by saying: 'It looks as if Lennox will be trying to get to Auckland thinking Becky was going straight home. If she turns up after he reaches you, you'll just have to confess to him that her mad, crazy cousin tried to save the situation by pretending she was Becky, but if she doesn't turn up, we may save it yet. Because surely she'll ring me here when she gets to Christchurch. She wouldn't leave me for long in ignorance of her whereabouts. If she does ring, I'll insist she comes back to swap places with me pronto.'

Aunt Mirrie took it so calmly Rebecca felt irritated. Of course *she* was a thousand miles from the situation. She even giggled a little, as if this was nothing more than a schoolgirl prank. She said, 'She's bound to ring me. I'll do something. Get her to get in touch with you, but if anyone else answers the phone to disguise her voice. I'll also tell her to go for the lick of her life to South Canterbury. Fairlie, you said? Rebecca, you must just play it along. I can't have that girl of mine breaking another engagement. No man will risk taking her on if he thinks she makes a habit of this. If Lennox turns up I'll simply say that you—I mean Becky, of course—was sorry she'd run away and went back. We just may redeem the situation yet. I'll not say a word to her father. He'd go right up in the air and it's the last thing he's supposed to do.'

Rebecca put the phone down, her mind a turmoil. She didn't know what to hope for. If Lennox came back instead of going on to Auckland, she'd have to make a clean breast of it. What a showdown that would be! If it happened, she just hoped she could confess it, grab her cases, get into that rental car and drive madly over the Rubicon. Pray God the river didn't rise.

She flew down peering into all the rooms to familiarise herself with them, opened and shut cupboards, tried to photograph the contents on her memory, hastily donned an apron that was probably Sylvie's and began peeling the vegetables Darroch had brought in. Thank heaven for that cold leg of mutton in the fridge! Her eyes lit on a bowl of what proved to be stewed apple. Another bonus. She knew where the flour and sugar were now. She'd rub butter in till it was crumbly, heat up the apple, spread the crumble over and brown it. Almost everybody liked that, and it was so colossally easy. The autocratic Darroch might mellow still further under food he didn't have to prepare himself.

She had the table set by the time she heard them coming. Another hurdle taken, because it had given her time to find everything. Robert didn't seem to be worrying much about her being here; Nan seemed very reserved ... she had probably known Becky didn't bother with children, and Andrew was too young to be much bothered. She turned to look at him struggling to undo the zipped sweater he'd had on under his parka and forbore to help, guessing his one aim in life would be to catch up on the abilities of his brother and sister. He looked up, caught her eye and as she smiled at him, he smiled back, a slow smile that started in his eyes before it reached the corners of his mouth, and culminated in one deep dimple cleaving his left cheek. She said, 'Goodness, Andrew, how like your uncle you are,' and added quickly, 'I hadn't noticed it before.'

The smile widened, 'I haven't got a rough chin like he has!'

His uncle laughed, swung him up, rubbed the rough chin against the smooth cheek and said, 'You will have one day, Andrew, when you're a high-country farmer and I'm dozing in that rocking-chair.'

Except that Andrew's eyes were blue, and his hair not quite so bleached, they were two of a kind. Andrew would have pent-house eyebrows too when he was in his thirties, and be a man of the tussocks and the mountain gorges.

Rebecca said, 'Odd how likenesses crop up.' Small talk made you feel more comfortable, made things seem more ordinary. 'I think it's interesting to see three children so unlike ... Robert so dark, Nan coppery, Andrew tussock-gold.'

He nodded, lifting a lid off a pan and looking satisfied. 'Rob's the image of his mother, and Nan is like our mother, her grandmother. We were the same as this family, all different. Even our twin sisters weren't like each other. Yet you say you have a cousin who often gets mistaken for you.'

Rebecca hoped her heightened colour would be put down to being so close to the hot stove. 'M'm, but our fathers are brothers and our mothers twins, so that explains it. But it's largely the colouring. Now, if everybody washes their hands, we'll dish up.'

Mention of Becky's cousin had so alarmed Rebecca it almost destroyed her appetite. She forced down what she could and only hoped she'd not develop ulcers, living under such a strain. Her mind seemed divided in two, one part full of apprehension, the other automatically responding to the children's chatter and Darroch's small talk. The latter sounded forced. She was sure he was trying to be cordial to a girl he despised, yet now must respect in a certain measure because she'd admitted she was at fault and was going to try to redeem the situation.

Rebecca's part lay in responding as to one whose house she'd supposedly lived in for weeks and not as to a newly-met stranger. But it wasn't easy. Andrew said, 'Who'll tell me my story tonight?' and she found herself saying, 'I will, of course. I'll just get the dishes washed up and I'll bath you and then we'll have a story-telling time without having to rush it.'

Andrew blinked, said, 'But you said you were no

earthly good at *tell* stories, you could only read them, and we didn't fink you even liked reading to us.'

She was conscious that Darroch's eyes were full of surprise too. She managed a laugh. 'Well, maybe I was shy about making up stories, but in an emergency I'll have a shot.'

Darroch said, 'Oh, was that it? I think we've done you less than justice. I can understand it because Ewan and Sylvie are so good at stories.'

'So are you,' said Nan. 'We like his stories of when he and Dad and our aunts were little.'

That gave Robert an idea. 'Becky, if you don't want to make up stories, you could tell us ones of when you were small and lived in all sorts of exciting countries. You must have had some great adventures.'

Nan was losing her reserve. 'Yes, like being in India with tigers and elephants and lions and ...'

Robert was scornful. 'No lions in India, stupid. Lions live in Africa. You *are* dumb!'

'Well, we were in Africa too,' said Rebecca recklessly, to save Nan's face, 'so that's what's got Nan mixed. Though the only lions I saw were in game reserves and I really haven't any exciting stories about them, because you see I only visited my parents there in school holidays. Most of the time I was in New Zealand with my aunt and uncle and their family.'

That reminded Nan. 'You and your cousin used to pretend you were each other to play tricks on people, didn't you?'

Oh, heavens! 'It only took in people who didn't know us very well. We wouldn't have got away with it at home. It was pretty stupid, anyway, making fools of people like that. We both got spanked for it once and deserved it, because we were dodging the blame for something at school. So I'd much rather forget past sins, and if there's going to be any telling of stories I'll have a shot at making them up.'

She thought of the stories she'd written for the children's section of her paper and thanked her lucky stars she'd been working in Auckland, not in the South, where they might have been recognised. There was a hazard every moment in a situation like this. Pray Heaven she didn't have to maintain it for more than two or three days. If only, if only Becky would ring her mother first before ringing here, so she could be warned what her cousin had done.

Darroch did nothing for her peace of mind by saying, as they rinsed and stacked the dishes for the dish-washer, 'When we've got the children down, I think you and I should have a long talk. We might be able to iron out a few of the problems that bugged you and Lennox. Don't say it's none of my business, because it seems as if it's the setting that upset you, and that *is* my business!'

That left her with nothing to say but, 'Thank you, Darroch. I'd appreciate that.' She went off with Andrew to the bathroom.

He enjoyed his bath so much and took such advantage of having a stranger to supervise it that she'd never have got him out if Darroch hadn't appeared and decreed he stop playing with the floating ducks and boats and allow himself to be dried. Rebecca's jersey and trews were plastered to her with soapy water, wet hair in strands hung about her face and the bathroom floor was awash.

Darroch Fordyce didn't look half so formidable when he burst out laughing. 'You should have got your hand in earlier, Becky, before you were landed with this. *Out*, Andrew! No more stramashing about.' He hauled him over the edge, stood him on a stool, wrapped an enormous towel about him.

Andrew protested. 'Grown-ups are mean! They're spoil-sports! Uncle, don't *you* ever push my boats round in *your* bath?'

Rebecca giggled, but Andrew's uncle didn't answer. They both looked at him. A reluctant grin struggled through. 'Now you've shamed me, young Andrew. Yes, I do, but you aren't to tell everyone. I'm quite glad you leave some down here at our place.'

Still less formidable. Rebecca's spirits began to rise. This family was fun. Perhaps it would be possible to get everything straightened out. At least they appeared able to see the funny side of everything.

'Becky, I'll take him off to the kitchen to dry ... I'll leave this mess to you to mop up ... just use the towels. Then you'd better get changed. Sorry about this. Kids always seize the chance to play up. His mother would have smacked his bottom long since.'

Rebecca sloshed round, called out to Nan to bring her some dry towels. Nan appeared in the doorway. 'What a duffer you are, you know the linen cupboard opens from here too,' and she whisked open a door disguised by a long mirror, to reveal piles of towels stacked against hot-waterpipes. Rebecca said feebly that she'd clean forgotten you didn't have to go right round to the hall for them.

Nan said in quite a kindly tone, 'Well, Mum said we had to make allowances for you, that you'd lived in so many places where servants would wait on you hand and foot that perhaps it was natural you were hopeless in the house. Oh, gosh, I suppose I shouldn't have said that. Don't ever tell Mum, will you, because she's trying to break me of the habit of being too outspoken. And I only said it now because you somehow seem different.'

Rebecca caught her breath. Nan plunged on. 'I mean, you're trying to help even if——' she stopped, said despairingly, 'There I go again!'

Rebecca twinkled at her, 'You mean even if I'm not very good at helping yet.'

Nan looked relieved. 'You—you don't mind me dropping bricks like that? It's hard not to. I like saying what I think.'

Rebecca gave her a hug. 'I was like that too when I

was a kid. Don't think another thing about it. It gets easier after a while because you realise that you don't like other people being too candid about yourself.'

Nan looked up at her, spreading a towel on a rail, said, 'You sure have changed. I'm sorry now I said that about you being a real stinker, but I was so mad when I heard you say to Uncle Lennox that I was an odious child and boarding-school'd do me all the good in the world.'

Rebecca felt appalled. Surely Becky hadn't gone as far as that in the child's hearing! No wonder she was unpopular. Now she herself was saddled with the reputation for saying such things. Things of which she was unaware. Oh, she'd have something to say to Becky when they met up again to switch roles! She'd try to create a new image, in the short time she'd be here, and make Becky see she must not upset this nice family whose way of life suited them! Perhaps she was being critical and smug, but Becky really could see only her own viewpoint. She must be made aware that making it up with Lennox was only part of it ... this lovely family deserved better treatment from her. Discord in an isolated property like this was unthinkable.

She found Nan was gazing at her intently. Perceptively too, as she found the next moment when the child said, 'You looked sorry about something. Why?'

Rebecca said slowly, 'I'm sorry I said that about you. I *was* a stinker. Evidently when I said I got over being too candid, I hadn't. As a grown-up I ought to have known better.'

'Lumme! I didn't think you'd ever apologise to a kid. I say, we don't have to tell Uncle Darroch about this, do we?'

'Don't have to tell Uncle Darroch what?' asked a voice from the doorway. His.

Nan looked alarmed.

Rebecca said calmly, 'Darroch, Nan and I didn't hit it off before. We've just apologised to each other for former hostilities, most of them my fault, and I don't think we need to discuss it further. It's over and done with.'

'Fair enough,' he said, 'hatchet buried. That could go for me too. Now, dry things. You can't sit on Andrew's bed like that. I've got him in. You other two can listen to Becky's story, then have your baths. I've things to do in my office.'

The office was right opposite the boys' room. Rebecca wished he'd shut the door between, but with the central heating system, doors weren't often shut here. From the lack of sound in there, shuffling of papers or opening of drawers, she had the distinct feeling he was listening too. Perhaps to see if this change of heart in Becky was going to continue.

Andrew looked a cherub, tucked in with a Teddy-bear one side, and a silky-looking ginger-and-white spaniel the other, who rejoiced in the name of Hector. 'You'll kiss him goodnight too, won't you?' asked Andrew anxiously. 'He gets his feelings hurt very easily. He likes to be kissed last of all, after Teddy. Me first.'

Robert said, '*I* wouldn't kiss that thing for anything. Andrew used to suck his nose when he was little.'

Andrew said indignantly, 'That was years ago. Mum's washed him lots and lots of times since.'

Robert jeered ... 'It's supposed to be machine-washable, but Andrew won't let Mum put him in the machine.'

Rebecca said, 'I shouldn't think she would. He ought to be done in the bath, same as you, Robert. Not even in a tub. Now are we going to have a story, or sit here arguing all night?'

Nan asked, 'Is this going to be a story for our age, or Andrew's age?'

Andrew's face went scarlet with anger. 'I can *so* understand older stories! *I* don't want fairy-stories and elves and pixies! I like stories about kids like us. And I'm catching up on you two every day, see. I'll soon be as old as you.'

It was too much for Nan and Robert, they sat back on their haunches and howled with laughter. 'Oh, you nit! You don't ever catch up. You can't. Nobody ever catches up in age.'

Rebecca held her grin back, said, 'But everybody has a lifetime, Andrew, and when *they're* getting really old, they'll be wishing they were as young as you.'

He looked thoughtful. The slow smile dawned, he said with glee, 'Yeah! You'll die before me. How'll you feel then?'

It was time, Rebecca knew, for a diversion. 'This story is about three children, about your own ages. And it tells how the littlest one of all was the one who found a priceless Maori canoe, all carved and ornamented, in a cave that had never been discovered before, on a lonely coast in the Far North of New Zealand....'

It was sheer inspiration. She didn't hustle to get it finished, because children always knew when you were dying to get back to fire or television. At the back of her mind, nevertheless, was the wish to be able to phone Aunt Mirrie again, now she knew the story and would realise Rebecca dared not give much away at this end. If she had heard from Becky, she might be able to tell her where she was, so Rebecca could get in touch, and if Becky had made any time for reaching Fairlie to swap identities.

She told Nan to go off to the bathroom first, was told by Robert that Andrew always said a little prayer, heard it, kissed him goodnight, hoped desperately this wouldn't be the time when he'd cry for his mummy, kissed Teddy and Hector, and was just about to turn out his light when the telephone in Darroch's office rang.

She stood as if turned to stone. It didn't have to be Becky. It didn't have to be her aunt. It could be anyone, even a wrong number. But it was a dreadful moment. If it was Becky, and Becky hadn't rung her mother first ... Oh, Rebecca knew she ought never to have succumbed to that moment of stupid temptation.

Then she heard Darroch say, 'Sylvie ... yours is the last voice I expected to hear! Oh, no operation till Friday? Well, it'll be a good thing over. Didn't it come on quickly? How are the kids? Oh, just fine. Sylvie, you'll never guess what, Becky had a change of heart and came back. She'd only got as far as Timaru, then hired a car and returned. You could have knocked me down with a feather. She seems a different person. She was appalled to hear you'd taken ill and is pitching in in great style.

'She cooked dinner, bathed Andrew, she and Nan have declared a truce, and she and I are going to have a heart-to-heart tonight when she finishes tucking the children down. She's told them a most entertaining story. I'd like to get this straightened out before Lennox gets back. I'm afraid he's on his way to Auckland, but she rang her mother this afternoon and seems to have every hope that her mother will put the situation to him very well. He's bound to respect her for coming back.

'Yes, yes, I know, Sylvie, I couldn't credit it, either. No, I'm not putting it on to ease your mind. It was like—like seeing a grub turn into a butterfly. Oh, that's a poor simile, because she was the butterfly first. It seems to me she's the flibberty-gibbet type, who comes up trumps in an emergency. I did wonder what in the world Lennox had seen in her, and dreaded disillusionment for him—he's so idealistic—but now I must admit to a certain admiration. It wasn't by any means easy, after writing a note like that, to admit to a mistake. It took guts. We'll have to meet her more than halfway. She's had a sort of luxurious, cosmopolitan life, and we're so used to our stark conditions here, I'm inclined to think now that we didn't make enough allowances. It must seem appallingly lonely to someone used to London, Paris, Toronto. All I want now is for Lennox to get back. I've never seen him in such a state as when he went off, have you?

'Anyway, girl,' he went on, 'the main thing is you've

nothing to worry about. This new Becky is pulling her weight and being very pleasant about it. I was going to get Meg over tomorrow—she's supposed to be back from her holiday. Poor Meg! But not now. This may not last, but I've a feeling it will. But I'll see the children don't suffer. One hint of anything that worries me and I'll get Meg across the water. I do wish we were nearer to visit you, Sylvie, it's just awful Ewan being away, but the Winmores and your other Timaru friends will be in and out to see you. I'll bring the children down for a visit when you're feeling up to them. Yes, I promise I won't let Ewan know. He'll be back about the time you're convalescing at Winmores. What a shock he'll get! Right ... we'll be thinking about you, Sylvie ... Night-night and God bless.'

Rebecca had been standing in the darkness of the hall, away from that open door, listening with all her might, and now she silently stole away, told Nan not to delay in the bath, so Robert, back in the kitchen, could get in. She wanted to ring her aunt while Darroch was still in his office. She sank thankfully into a chair. What a day! Only sheer determination had carried her on.

As soon as Robert was in the bath she went along to the office, poked her head round the door, said, because she didn't want him lifting his receiver while she was on the phone, 'I'm going to give my mother a ring to see if Lennox has reached there yet.'

He gave her quite an understanding smile. 'Naturally you'd like to speak to him yourself in private. I won't come out till you give me the all-clear, and I'll see to getting Robert and Nan tucked down.' He hesitated, said, 'Don't feel too badly about this. I don't—quite—know how Lennox will react. Do try to understand if he seems as mad as a meat-axe at first, that it will be because he flew all that way on a wild-goose chase, only to have you come back to Craigievar. But I'm sure his second reaction will be to give you credit for being big enough to

come back. If he bawls you out too much, hand him over
to me. If he knows I'm glad you came back and can say
you're working well in this emergency, it may soothe
him down. But of course, don't forget he may only have
got as far as Christchurch, may not have been able to get
a booking till tomorrow morning. If so, I hope to God he
rings here first.'

Rebecca thought hollowly, 'And *I* hope to God he
doesn't! I need time to get that wretched Becky back to
Fairlie. It's my only hope. I could kill her going off like
that. And to be quite honest with myself, I deserve to be
whipped for pretending to be her when Darroch thought
I was!'

She got through to Aunt Mirrie. There had been no
word from Becky, no word from Lennox. And to make
things easier up there, Uncle Alan had gone off for a
couple of nights to his sister's holiday house at Whanga-
paroa. Wasn't that lucky? Well, if it was, thought
Rebecca sourly, it was the first piece of luck in the whole
affair. But yes, Uncle Alan wasn't going to be pleased
about any of this. And who could blame him? Aunt
Mirrie finished up, 'Just play it along, darling. We might
yet come out of it without anyone knowing you took her
place. I dread another broken engagement. Alan said,
when she was so determined to become engaged to Lennox, that if she broke this one off, she was on her own
financially, that she could buckle down and get a job not
in his office, earn her own keep. That she'd had things
too easily too long, that we'd spoilt her and if she wanted
to go on through life breaking engagements and upsetting
nice young men, she was out on her own. I'd never heard
him speak to Becky like that before. Anyway, Rebecca,
even if you did have to confess to this Darroch Fordyce
that you aren't Becky, he can't eat you, especially if you
pull your weight in the household in this emergency.'

All very well for Aunt Mirrie, thought Rebecca despairingly again, as she put the phone down. *She* was a thousand miles away.

Darroch came in, reported the children asleep, pulled the simmering kettle on to the hottest part of the range, made them coffee, brought out a tin of biscuits, put some on a wooden platter, sat down in the opposite chair and said, 'Now, let's talk.'

Rebecca's stomach felt like a ball of knotted twine below her midriff. One wrong word and she was for it.

'You've got to be very sure this time, Becky. From your note you said if Lennox loved you enough he'd get Aunt Davy to put money into a farm nearer the coast and the cities. That just won't happen. It's high-country or nothing with my aunt. But remember that if she does buy this in, an area from both the Richards and the Greenwoods, then we could have complete access by road, *in time*. It won't be long before there's this bridge open between Dragonshill and Heronscrag, and that track does link us with Heronscrag. But it needs a mighty lot of upgrading ... at our expense ... before it can be called a road. I'm sure Len will have told you all this when he took you to Heronscrag. Did he? Surely? It's important.'

She said uncertainly, 'I can't—quite—remember. You mean if I persuade Lennox to farm nearer the cities, it will deprive the rest of you of this access? But yours is such a shallow ford, and not even very wide. And never quicksands such as the Pawerawera has after flood. That must have been terrible. A good job Dragonshill has a bridge now, leading to the new ski-fields.' (That much she was safe to say.)

'Never quicksands? What—who—gave you that idea? There are quicksands in all these rivers after floods. I don't want you to think we'd put any pressure on you, about Aunt Davina buying in this property, because it would help us, I'm only trying to tell you that in time, if you came to live here, the isolation mightn't be quite so complete. All women have fears, naturally, about terrain like this. They usually go down-country well beforehand to have their babies, but dread illness for themselves or their children and menfolk, at times when we're cut off by the flooded river. The Heronscrag Bridge will relieve some of that anxiety, but we could still be cut off by snow. I've got to put the complete picture before you. The one consolation now is that in times of real emergency, helicopters can usually, though not always, get in. That's why I felt you must come to live here before you marry Lennox. No good waiting till the knot's tied. Can you face it, Becky?'

She looked across at him, in the rather dim light in the kitchen. It was a face all planes and angles, with cheekbones and brow structure thrusting through as the rocks in this rugged terrain did. It was weatherbeaten, tanned, ruddy, with deeply scored laughter lines at each side of his eyes so that when his face wasn't smiling, the grooves were whiter in the tan. A high-bridged nose gave him an arrogant look and he had a jaw to match that. She could imagine Becky being terrified of him. She liked sleek, suave men, given to facile compliments.

He was gazing at the red glow of the range, perhaps to let her take her time to answer, but now he felt her eyes on him and looked at her. 'Have I made it sound too harsh, Becky? Would Lennox think I've overdone it? Though it's hard to draw *too* harsh a picture. You see, it's been a mild winter, for the first time for years. So since you've been here, we've not had our usual share of hardship and crisis. But whatever Lennox may have felt about playing it down, I don't. But it's an odd thing. While all women who've lived here have, at times, hated the elements, had their moments of rebellion, I don't know one who hasn't come to love it, as their men did, not one who hasn't left her heart behind when the time came to retire. One, of course, never could leave it. I think Sylvie was telling you about old Madame Beaudonais who died last year at the age of a hundred and two. She lived up here in days of extreme peril and tough endurance, and lived to see the Pawerawera bridged. The River-of-Dread.

'But perhaps the most remarkable is Joanna Greenwood, as you know. Imagine being secretary to a London TV star, and falling for the owner of Heronscrag! Not only that, but she fell in love with Heronscrag itself first. Lennox had great hopes of you because of her. Deal gently with my young cousin, Becky, but remember, if you decide to stay, it must be for keeps. Can you take it? Think about it in great depth, and if you can't take it, say so before you take the irrevocable step of marriage and ruin Len's life.'

Now Rebecca knew in full the enormity of what she'd done in a moment of foolish impulsiveness. She'd raised hopes that ought not to have been raised and because of that she was being asked a question that only her cousin could answer.

She kept her head bent. Her heart was thudding. What dare she say? She was a stupid, heedless girl, whose ridiculous vanity, fostered by the memory of having helped her cousin out of scrapes time and time again had led her into this and snarled up the lives of people who, till now, had been content with their lives.

Without looking up she said, 'Darroch, I just don't know. Give me time. I must try to work things out, try myself out. Lennox will be back soon. Leave it till then. There isn't any great rush to decide, is there? I mean, about your aunt buying in the property?'

'No, it's not on the market, just at the early discussion stage between the three properties. Aunt Davina is in America just now, as you know. Good job she's coming back by ship. Like Lennox, she loves the sea and is taking a cruise on the way home round the islands.'

A faint hope stirred in Rebecca. If Lennox loved the sea, might he not, after all, be happier on a coastal farm, with access to the ocean?

'Well, thank you for this talk, Darroch,' she said. 'I'll pull my weight while Sylvie's away. Just help me all you can to find my feet. If I seem a bit bumbling, do try to understand I'm a novice at housekeeping' (this was for Becky's sake when she was smuggled in here again) 'and when Lennox gets back, if he's as understanding as you've been, we might just get by.'

'I'm inclined to think there's a good chance ... now. I wonder if I ought to explain Lennox to you a little. You hardly know each other, after all. You said in your note —do forgive me for quoting it, but in his misery Len showed it to me—you said it looked as if you were the one who had to make all the sacrifices, that he was making none.

'You couldn't know, but at the time he didn't want to make you feel he'd missed out on something that had been a dream for a long time. I said he loves the sea. Before he met you at Ruapehu, he had the chance of joining three fellows on a yacht going round the islands. We thought he ought to get you here pronto to see the place under winter—or late winter—conditions. Not just in summer, because the summers here are glorious. He agreed, not without a struggle, and never told you. He won't get the chance again once he's married. So—both of you must learn to give and to take. The sacrifice wasn't all on your side, Becky.'

He saw the silver glimmer of tears in the dark blue eyes, said, 'Don't cry, Becky. It will all come out in the wash, but remember this. Len's a good deal younger than I. I know only too well that when I was younger I was more likely to lose my block over something like this. His very love for you may make him more awkward, more sensitive. He may feel you've made a fool of him. But I'll have a word with him first if at all possible. He's bound to be back soon.'

In which he was quite, quite wrong.

Next morning the children were in the schoolroom, settled there by Darroch, even Andrew, who was colouring in, and Rebecca was preparing the morning tea their uncle had said he'd come out for at ten, when the phone rang.

She rushed to answer. How lucky ... if this was Becky or Lennox she'd get the conversation over before Darroch emerged from the schoolroom. It was neither. It was the local post office ... if anything a score of miles off could be called local ... and they were ringing up a telegram. When she had taken it down and had it read over for absolute accuracy, she dropped into a seat and buried her head in her hands, her brain numb.

Darroch found her like that three minutes later. He stared. 'What is it? Don't—don't tell me Lennox has rung and is so furious to find you back here when he's been chasing all over New Zealand that he's blasted your ears off?'

Her lips felt so stiff she could hardly frame the words. She shook her head instead, swallowed, then managed to say, 'No, but there's a telegram from him. From Tauranga.'

'Tauranga? What the hell's he doing in Tauranga? Here, let me read it for——'

'No ... you couldn't read it. I took it down in shorthand. I—I'll read it to you.'

It was quite a long telegram. He'd evidently tried to be guarded enough so that evidences of an upset relationship weren't apparent to the local staff. Rebecca gulped and read slowly as she interpreted her shorthand. 'Changed my mind about keeping that appointment in Auckland stop have accepted that decision as final so diverted to Tauranga to say farewell to shipmates and succumbed to their request to accompany them after all stop we sail at dawn tomorrow stop it shouldn't inconvenience you with Ewan expected home so soon stop will ring from Fiji regards to all Len.'

'Hell and damnation!' roared Darroch. 'I'll stop him somehow. What *was* the name of that flaming boat? The *Oleander*? No. Um—The *Jacaranda*? No, I know ... The *Hibiscus*. Must be some sort of marine office there ... I'll ring the harbourmaster. That's it. Away from that phone, Becky and let me get at it. He mustn't sail without knowing you're here.'

'It's no good,' said Rebecca in a strange, high voice. 'It's no good. I asked what time it was handed in. He put it in up there too late for it to reach the office here by last night. They've sailed this morning. It serves me right, Darroch. It's all my fault.' But how much fault there was, he couldn't know.

CHAPTER THREE

REBECCA wouldn't have blamed Darroch Fordyce if he'd let loose a string of shepherd's curses, if he'd ripped a piece off her for triggering off this situation, but his appalled silence was even more dreadful. She felt bereft of speech, even of power of feeling. What *had* she got herself into?

Then he came to, said sharply as he took in her blanched cheeks, the very real fear in her eyes, 'Don't look like that. Don't flake out on me. Let's—let's just get our breath back.'

She said indignantly, 'I'm not likely to flake out. I don't—ever. Modern girls don't have the vapours! But I almost wish I could at the moment. I'm the one who's brought this on Craigievar and I couldn't have picked a worse time. Sylvie facing an operation tomorrow and Ewan overseas. Lennox would never have done this but for me.' For one incredible moment she felt as if she was in very truth Becky. As if she was the one who'd run away and caused Lennox to do the same. He must have been distraught.

The big man in front of her sensed her agony of mind and most unexpectedly smiled at her, sat down, took her hands, said, 'Becky, it's the oddest thing, but in some ways I feel better about Len than before. I don't think anything but the most devastating candour is going to serve. I've been desperately worried about Len, about his coming marriage to you. Women of the high-country don't have it easy, ever, but if their love for the men they choose is overriding, they'll take anything. Until this moment I didn't feel you cared enough for my young cousin. But now, seeing you like this, I couldn't doubt you cared. Care to the point of agonising over the situation. Not just for the pair of you, but even for the work of the station. We ought to have been more patient with you, ought to have sensed that under your—um—critical attitude, you were homesick and scared. I've seen you in a new light since you've come back. I wish Sylvie and Ewan had too, but they will yet.

'It doesn't matter about Len because he probably fell in love with the real you from the start and knew you could come right again. Look, it'll do Lennox good to have a complete break. He's always wanted to do a trip like this, so he'll get it out of his system. He'll have cooled off long before he gets to Fiji and when he contacts us I'll let him know you came back in an emergency and did a darned good job. Oh, I know it's early days, but I'm confident you'll stick to it. So don't worry—or if that's impossible, don't worry overmuch! Everyone up here seems to have a stormy courtship . . . Penny, Verona, Joanna, Henrietta. It's stormy country! They all got their wires crossed somewhere, but unravelled them in the end.'

(But you've no idea, Darroch Fordyce, how ravelled *these* lines are! Ravelled beyond hope of untangling, at that!)

His eyes demanded she buck up. She managed a philosophical look as if his words had solaced her. His hands were still covering her cold ones. She freed them, drew back, said a little shakily, 'Well, we can do nothing just now. If Lennox is on the high seas, he's out of touch with our world. There's nothing to do but get on with the job in hand, which at the moment is calling the children to their playtime, and then getting back to lessons.'

'I'll relieve you of that this morning. You can do the dinner. I'll gladly hand over that chore.'

Her mind was a treadmill with thoughts scurrying endlessly round. She took a packet of beef mince out of the deep freeze as they'd forgotten to get something out last night. She thanked her lucky stars that at least you could start that off from frozen. She peeled vegetables from the cold store, dug deep into the still hard ground, and put on a very easy steamed pudding that took only an hour and a half. If Darroch thought anything about it, seeing Becky had done very little cooking here, he'd think she'd simply swotted up a recipe book, not putting it down to expertise gained in editing the *Chronicle*'s cookery pages. After some hideous mistake once, it was a rule to test all recipes ahead. Children weren't madly keen on steamed puddings as a rule, but if she made a butterscotch sauce with it they'd probably down it in great style, and men loved them. She thought Darroch Fordyce deserved a decent dessert! For forbearance if nothing else.

It was a great success with them all. Darroch took two helpings. 'Make this for my men some time. They come off the hill with gargantuan appetites after days of basic food of their own hashing. You're discovering things about yourself, aren't you? I could swear you've got a glow of pride out of producing a dinner like this. Keep it up, lass. The way to a man's heart is supposed to be through his stomach, and even if Len was flaming mad when he took off, if he thinks you're responding like this to the challenge of being the only woman on the station, he'll think he's pretty lucky . . . glamour *and* capability!'

Rebecca managed a feeble smile. 'I've been lucky in what I've attempted so far, aided by the cookbooks. There could be rocks ahead, biscuits like concrete and many burnt offerings . . . don't count too many chickens.'

Nan beamed, 'Isn't it funny? We all like you better now, Becky. But what do you mean, Uncle, about Uncle Len being mad?'

Her uncle got up, said, 'Well, before I drop any more clangers, back to the schoolroom. Just that Uncle Len was a bit fed up with farm life, so he's going on that yacht after all.' He added, 'Don't bother to go with the children, Becky, I'll get them settled and come back to help you clear up.'

'No, stay with them but leave Andrew with me. He's been an angel-child this morning and when I'm through I'll take him for a walk. It will do both of us good.'

He grinned. 'You could easily feel better for some fresh air after this wallop from Fate.'

As she gazed after him she thought despairingly that he was being so decent about everything, it only made it harder to bear! If only she hadn't embarked on this stupid deception . . . it was getting harder every moment to confess. But there was still a chance of getting Becky back, and, given enough time in Fairlie, making her see that if she was prepared to pull her weight here she might still save her engagement.

Access was going to be easier if Aunt Davina bought that land, and they could have a modern house with every convenience built. That mountain road or track would connect with the bridges at Heronscrag and Dragonshill so that flood wouldn't maroon them. Possibly too, with a better skiing season than this year, Becky might find great compensations. The crowds at the new ski-field had departed by the time she'd arrived, but this had been a freakishly mild winter. There was always gaiety and social life at a ski-field. It needn't be all tough farming routine such as Becky had found. Poor Lennox, when he found her so good at snow sports, he must have thought he'd found the ideal wife for alpine farming, not knowing it was the more sophisticated life of the winter seasons in Norway, Austria and Switzerland that appealed to Becky.

Andrew was the most engaging companion and loved having a grown-up all to himself. He was remarkably knowledgeable and observant for his age. He could see movements everywhere, so could point out birds in darting or soaring flight, the swift slither of a lizard, disturbed at warming itself against the sun-warm boulder, and even discerned a thar, high on one of the crags, long before Rebecca could focus to distinguish it from its surroundings. He prattled away about deer, chamois, mountain goats, and Rebecca thankfully absorbed it all, because he wasn't as likely as the others to remark on how interested she was now, from at first.

Then he surprised her by saying, 'Isn't it funny what a duffer you used to be about these things, but you're learning fast, aren't you?'

They picked up driftwood, water-torn into weird and wonderful shapes by mountain torrents, to join the vast collection at the house, and dozens of gloriously coloured stones for the schoolroom collection. 'We'll take these back to our own schoolroom when Mummy comes home.'

The scenery was breathtaking. These southern heights were tremendous. They soared, glittering and remote, to lose themselves against an infinitude of sky, and below them the lesser spurs and ridges, all Craigievar property, were scarred and carved by aeons of exposure to fearsome elements into shapes that seemed to hold personalities of their own.

'Over there,' said Andrew, pointing with a dimpled forefinger, 'those funny rock-tops belong to Dragonshill and Heronscrag. The Witches' Cauldron, that lot is called ... not real witches, Becky, so you don't have to be scared. But 'lectric storms play over there and look like flames leaping up round a camp-fire pot. And Thunderclap Peak and where you can see four pointy ones, that's Richards' place, Four Peaks. But these ones here are ours. That's Ogre's Chute, a very bad shingle-fan. It moves very easily. We don't let the sheep string out across there if we can help it. No, sir! An' Sheerfall is that sawn-off-looking cliff face. Nobody is allowed to come down on that from the top at mustering, because it can have black ice on it and you can't see black ice on dark rock, did you know that, Becky? One step on that, and whoops, you'd be over the edge. Aunt Davy's husband lost a couple of sheep and a dog over there once.'

Rebecca was loving this, not only for the little earnest face and the endearing stamp, quite unmistakable, of a mountain man in the making, but because if she asked Darroch to point out and name these features for her he might say, 'But we named them for you when you first arrived.'

She kept an eye on the time, and presently suggested they should get back. 'I want you to go into the schoolroom and do some colouring-in because I'm making a surprise for afternoon tea,' so he went in quite amicably and shouted out about the surprise to come, to his uncle, who was hearing reading, and who asked, 'Do I share in this, and stay out?'

She grinned, 'Right, I'll make you one too,' and went off to the kitchen. But first she was going to ring her aunt and acquaint her with the fact that Lennox was now somewhere in the Pacific and incommunicado! And ask had Becky rung and left a number where Rebecca could contact her.

Aunt Mirrie had nothing to report. 'I'm afraid she knows what I'll say to her about running out on the Craigievar folk like this, so she'll dodge getting in touch as long as possible. Try to play it along for two or three days more, Rebecca, then if we don't hear, I'm afraid you'll just have to confess to this Darroch person who you are and why you did it. If he only knew you as well as we do, he'd realise you did it from the best possible motives. I've had to tell your uncle, and he's so fed up with her. I do hope it doesn't lead to a real breach between them. He says she's positively irresponsible—this was exactly what he feared, that there'd be another broken engagement, and he'll give her a piece of his mind when she does turn up. If only she'd ring and I could persuade her to go to Fairlie, change places with you, and try to make a go of it, it might all simmer down,' she sighed. 'If Alan thought she'd have a shot at it, he might feel differently. I had to give up so much of my daughter when she was young, at school in New Zealand, and I'm afraid if it comes to a real showdown between her and her father, she could clear off and I'd never see her again.

'Last year I had high hopes, before we came home. There was this young New Zealand aide in London. They were so attracted to each other, I thought it had gone really deeply with Becky this time. The odds were more in favour too, practically speaking. He could have given her the life she's used to, travel and excitement; I feel he'll go a long way. But they quarrelled. I'm sorry about all this, Rebecca, but for everyone's sake, do try to play it along a little more.'

Rebecca hung up, feeling miserable. There was nothing she could do. The most maddening thing always was when there was no action to be taken. Becky had vanished into thin air, and since she herself had been scatty enough to plunge into pretence there was nothing to do but carry on. Now she was committed to her surprise afternoon tea for three o'clock. Good thing pikelets were quick and easy.

She put her heavy frying-pan on the stove ... they might have a girdle, but she'd not seen one. She greased it, whipped up eggs and milk, sifted flour and baking soda and cream of tartar, added sugar and finally a little warmed butter and golden syrup, beat her batter, then dropped spoonfuls on the hot greased pan surface. Bubbles rose quickly, she flipped it over—ah, that was just right, nicely browned, so she could go ahead with more. She made a few ordinary round pikelets first, then carefully made pikelet men, adding a head, legs, arms. They turned out quite well, so she experimented, made rabbits and cats. She'd just finished when the children streamed out from the schoolroom.

Rebecca felt like an artist whose picture was being

praised. 'But lift the cats very carefully. Their tails are so thin they'll fall off otherwise. My mother used to say they'd turn into Manx cats when that happened.'

Darroch said, 'This is what I call going the second mile, not only hoeing into the housekeeping, but adding bonus points for the kids. Thanks.'

Every time he praised the changed Becky, Rebecca felt a hypocrite. She mustn't overdo things. But she was discovering in herself the strongest, strangest urge to stand well in this man's eyes. If it came to a showdown, if Becky failed to turn up, if she herself failed to redeem this situation, would he count it to the credit side that at least she had tried to keep them in comfort while they were shorthanded or would her thoughtless masquerade make him so furious, he'd wipe the floor with her and send her packing, vowing he never wanted to see either herself or her cousin again?

Worst, how was Lennox going to react? Would this Pacific cruise have the effect of cooling him off and softening towards the errant Becky? Would he want to rush home, perhaps fly, and make it up? She had no answer to these tormenting questions, only a hollow scared feeling. The children ran out to play.

She almost jumped when Darroch said, 'I'm worried about that rental car. It's just sitting here eating money. But I can't leave this place to follow you to Fairlie when Sylvie's being operated on. I want to be within reach of the phone, but we must try to get it back the following day.'

She said quickly, 'I got it through someone I knew—so strange to find him in Timaru. He let me have it at a reduced price for a week. So if I got it back too soon, it wouldn't benefit me. I'd have to pay the dearer rate for a shorter time.' She was becoming a practised liar and hated herself for it.

Darroch's voice was surprised. 'Why a week when you were just coming back here?'

Her mind worked with lightning rapidity. 'Well, I was so scared you wouldn't have me back, I thought if you wouldn't, I'd drive on to Mount Cook and Queenstown before going home. I felt my parents would be furious with me too.'

Darroch said slowly, 'But these things happen. Better a broken engagement than a broken marriage. Surely parents wouldn't——' he broke off and his eyes narrowed. 'Unless you've made a habit of this! You haven't, have you? Because then I could understand parents being annoyed. They'd never know where they were.'

Rebecca felt confused, caught on the hop. She was trying to build up a better image for Becky. She said lamely, 'Well ... I was so much younger, didn't know my own mind. I——'

His mouth curled, his voice was derisive. 'Didn't know your own mind then? What makes you think you know it now?' He got up, strode off, paused at the doorway to say over his shoulder, 'I think it's just as well my young cousin's beyond communication at this moment. You'd both be better for longer consideration. I don't want any quick making-up.'

The humiliation of it stayed with Rebecca. She had no heart for the evening meal. She took frozen soup out of the deep-freeze, did toast with it, put out cheese and apples and some shortbread Sylvie must have cooked. Darroch made an effort to sound normal, for the children's sakes, she guessed, but she sensed he found it a strain. She wished it hadn't happened when he was worried about his sister-in-law and what she was facing on the morrow.

She found it hard going herself. She played an extended game of Ludo with the children, one she thought would never end and which caused umpteen wrangles, supervised baths, read, told stories, felt unutterably weary and depressed. She was afraid of the morrow too, not only because of Sylvie but because the men would be coming off the hill before sundown. There wouldn't be just one man to deceive, but four. One unguarded moment and she'd be unmasked. Oh, Becky, ring, ring, before it's too late!

She put off the lights, hoped desperately that they'd go to sleep pronto instead of coming wide awake as children sometimes did, arriving out for drinks of water, with stories of hearing 'things that go bump in the night', visits to toilet, not being able to find Teddy-bears which had slipped down between bed and wall, having a tickly nose ... she'd had endless experience of that sort of caper with her brother's children.

In that, at least, she was lucky. Silence reigned. She made herself some black coffee, cut a slice of ginger-bread, tried to read a book. Finally she got interested in it: *Mary of Carisbrook*. The magic of reading, as always, gripped her, beguiling her away from this grim present where she'd got herself into a ghastly situation, where she couldn't respect herself any more.

Suddenly she was thirteen thousand miles away, in a castle on the Isle of Wight, and time had slipped back three hundred years, with a king who knew his life was at stake, who was agonisingly concerned about his family, a king whose one hope of escape lay in a plan that depended wholly upon a favourable tide. Imagine had that happened now, all he'd have needed was a motor-launch, not a wind set fair for France!

It was mad to be reading a story of Charles the First and finding yourself still hoping for that favourable tide despite your knowledge of the facts of history! Margaret Campbell Barnes was doing the impossible ... keeping up suspense even when you knew what had really happened, when you knew that this story had been written in blood three centuries ago, in England's most shameful hour when the foulness of regicide had stained the pages of history.

The words blurred before her, she made a tiny sound,

half gasp, half sob ... felt impatiently for her handker-chief, then Darroch Fordyce's voice said, 'I'm sorry. Don't cry. I was too rough on you—and I don't know the circumstances of that other broken engagement.'

So strong was the spell of the story upon her that she looked up at him uncomprehendingly, her dark blue eyes starry with tears. She looked woefully tired, the red hair and dark brows standing out vividly against her pallor.

Then she blinked, said, 'Oh, that ... Oh, thank you for saying sorry, Darroch, and I'm sure I deserved what you said earlier, but——' her face flushed vividly in direct contrast to a moment before, 'you'll think me incredibly sentimental. I was crying over this book. I—couldn't help it. It makes me feel I want to set time back, to change the course of history. To have Charles the First escape from the Isle of Wight.'

He gazed at her, picked up the book, recognised it as one of his, and said, 'You mean so he escaped White-hall?'

She said, 'Yes, because he wasn't a wicked king, only foolish. And he'd had a foolish father, and I remember that because he was the second son he'd never been groomed or trained to be king. He was a kind father and a faithful husband, in days when they were scarce in royal circles ... oh, it's so ridiculous, but I felt tonight as if it were a personal loss and a personal shame. History always got me at school, but I never in my life felt so badly as tonight. That's artistry, I suppose ... on the part of the author?'

He nodded, looking down on the book. 'I've read all her historical novels, or most, but this is my favourite, though it *is* a painful experience reading it, knowing the end. I bought this on the Isle of Wight before visiting Carisbrook, so it was almost too vivid. It came alive for me, as my hand rubbed along that wall where he used to gaze from ... in the direction of France.'

(She must be careful. She didn't know he'd been to Britain. He and Becky might have exchanged similar travel experiences.)

He went on, 'And of course you've been to Windsor Castle ... I suppose you felt as I did, that one of the most poignant things to think about in St George's Chapel was to know that beneath your feet that body and head lay. To be told about the black velvet pall getting sprinkled with snow as they hurried him to his burial there is a moving experience.'

Rebecca knew of it, and forced herself to say, 'Yes, a pile like that, begun in the Conqueror's day, knows so much of glory and sadness.'

'Yes ... perhaps I ought to mutter that you shouldn't dwell on such morbid things, but it seems to me it would be a pity if we couldn't, in our easier existence, spare a thought for those of other times. Doesn't Wordsworth say something about "Old, unhappy far-off things, and battles long ago." You're the most surprising person. I'd not have dreamed you'd care.'

She was getting into deep waters. A quick exchange with her cousin's identity might have been all right, but living at close quarters like this, being yourself, not your lightweight cousin, was coming to the top. She must be more careful ... go in for the gay, inconsequential, often amusing chatter that was Becky's. Being a newspaper-woman made you inclined to pursue certain topics, plunge into all sorts of conversations, analyse, sift. It wouldn't do in this situation. Oh, heaven send it didn't have to last long!

Darroch pulled the kettle on. 'I'll make our last cuppa fairly early tonight. Tomorrow night, with the men back, we could be much later. After so many early nights, because there are only storm-lanterns up there, in the huts, they'll want to make a bird of it on T.V. and there's that late Rugby match they'll want to watch on the colour set. They've just got black-and-white in their quarters.

We'll have to get them a colour one soon. How would you like me to do bacon strips and cheese on toast?'

'I'd love it,' said Rebecca, immensely grateful not to be still at outs. What a domestic scene this was ... how strange that she should feel so content here, in a world very far removed from the newspaper one. She ought to be fretting to get on with that caravan life she had planned, following the career of her heart and choosing. She'd planned it so long, peace of mind and uninterrupted solitude in which to do her writing.

On the heels of that came the thought that *this* would be a wonderfully inspirational setting in which to put pen to paper. There was a magic about it, an invigorating sense of challenge.

Her gaze swept round the huge kitchen. Even this room was crammed with books. In every room in the homestead you were reminded that in the early days the pioneers had depended almost wholly upon reading for entertainment. Quite evidently they would read their favourites over and over again. Mail-days would be great events, when someone had ridden to Tekapo for the mail-bag. Sometimes, of course, they'd be cut off for weeks without news, in time of flood or snowfall. No television, no telephone, no radio. So books had been a necessity, not a luxury, sent out in bulk by ship, ordered months, sometimes a year or more earlier.

Other evidences reminded one ... the cupboard full of tattered music, and the old piano, still well tuned; the dainty watercolours on the walls, the pencil sketches, the carvings speaking of long hours of convalescence, often; the collections of photographs that portrayed the life on the station in all phases and decades. What greathearts there must have been among those pioneers. This was soft living compared to that. But the books Rebecca loved most. She'd liked to spend a lifetime here reading them.

A lifetime? What on earth was she thinking? Then it

swept over her, a knowledge she couldn't refute ... a knowledge she didn't want to face. *This was the one spot on earth in which she'd like to spend the rest of her life.* She looked across at Darroch Fordyce, his back to her, bending over his oven tray ... *and there was the man she'd like to spend that life with.* The utter hopelessness of it hit like a blow ... by her own folly she'd ruined any chance of a happy ending for herself. Once she got Becky back here, he must never know that for a few days, someone else had taken her place and found in him everything kindred she'd ever hoped for in a man.

CHAPTER FOUR

She was careful to keep the talk light while they had their snack. He held open the door for her to precede him up the passage and turned out the kitchen light. At that instant there was a flash and a white light, like the beam of a searchlight, lit the entire room for a split second then left them in darkness that seemed twice as dark as before. Rebecca cried out, alarmed, and clutched Darroch's arm.

'It's all right—just an electrical storm. We often get them in the mountains. Only that was dramatic because we'd just switched off. They're splendid to watch, even if disastrous at times in their effects. Come on up to the Lookout, it's the best place.'

Lookout? Where did he mean? She'd be supposed to know. He said, 'Come on, or are you too tired?'

'No, I'd like to see it.'

He pushed past her then, and she followed him along the passage to the very end where it turned the corner to his room and one other. At the very end was a door she'd supposed was another linen press or cloak-cupboard. He'd switched the light on, and it showed a narrow wooden stair. 'You can see your way by this light. You can switch the Lookout one on from here, but it spoils the effect.'

He put a hand back for hers, to help her up. She was acutely conscious of the warmth of his and of the feelings that were sweeping over her. This then was love. And there was danger in it. She was enough of a creature of impulses without having to reckon with this.

At the top he said, 'Keep hold of my hand and you won't fall over anything. It's full of lumber, I'll admit, but not in the centre.'

They came to a square uncurtained window and there before them was a magnificent sight. Rebecca was spellbound. 'It's over the Witches' Cauldron, isn't it?'

'Yes, we get other storms playing among other peaks, but it's always more spectacular when it brews there. Look at that now ... !'

An unearthly light lit the whole scope of their vision, outlining peaks with an intensity of revelation. Rays shot up in flashes and bursts, sulphur yellow, as if forced out of the cauldron with evil gases, fiery green, and eerie blue, flame and saffron and that ghostly, searching white.

'That thunder's echoing back from Thunderclap Peak. Hear the echo at the end of each roll?'

She said, laughing, standing close to him because the window was so small, 'You're almost exulting in it.'

He laughed, said apologetically, 'I can't help it even though it makes a tough situation tougher still.'

'Meaning?'

'Meaning that when it's over the Cauldron, we get cut off from civilisation. Come morning the Rubicon won't be able to be crossed, even on horseback, Becky. When Lennox gets back, if he hears you could even take being marooned, he'll know you've got what it takes after all. He'll have to admit that, even if he was madder than mad with you when he rushed off on that cruise.'

Her voice almost faded. 'But won't it be just a flash flood, as quickly up as it takes the water to reach here, and as quickly down?'

His tone was strange, deliberate. 'That's a storm of some magnitude. In flat areas, that would mean devastating floods. Here the river can contain it all, but it'll be four times its size and even though it rushes away, rain like that loosens the snow, and long after the whole catchment area has stopped draining in, the snow will crash, and thaw. I'd say two weeks before the Rubicon is fordable. Do you find that too appalling?'

She had to keep playing this part, she *had* to. She had

to be Becky, till that moment came, when come it surely must, and the real Becky could be brought to Fairlie to take on. She bit her lip till it hurt. She was glad of the darkness, but she couldn't control a shudder.

Darroch felt it. He slipped an arm round her shoulders in a comforting gesture. It meant nothing more, she knew. He hugged her.

'Bear up! It always goes down some time or other. It will give you a splendid chance to prove yourself. I'd never have believed I could come round to thinking you right for here, but I have. And so must Lennox when he hears, as he will hear it from me.'

She didn't answer—she couldn't. All she wanted to do was to burst into tears, cling to him, tell all. But she mustn't. There could be two weeks to go.

She pulled herself a little together, released her grip of him. 'Sorry about this. I've never been isolated before, you see. I felt appalled. But I'll make it, I guess. I must just think of those first women who lived up here. They didn't have even a phone.'

'Good girl! That's the way to look at it. I must get the others to ring you. You'll feel so different if you can yarn once in a while to Penny, Henrietta, Verona, and Joanna. Especially Joanna. She's our nearest neighbour and the pluckiest because of her background; you know from your visit there that she knows a number of the places you know.'

Rebecca could have bitten her tongue out. The less contact she had with anyone who'd known her cousin, the better, even over the phone. So far she'd not got tripped up with Darroch, but one lapse of memory as it would seem, or slip of the tongue with others she'd talked with, and she could be betrayed.

He took her hand again for the stairs. She moved quite abruptly away from him at the foot. He stopped at the door of his own room. She could see her way to hers. He said, 'Goodnight, Becky,' then, 'Doesn't anyone ever call you Rebecca? Becky is a name for a little girl. Rebecca would suit you much more.'

She felt herself shake a little. She'd love to hear her proper name on his lips. She dared not say she'd had to be Becky to distinguish her from her cousin Rebecca at school. She didn't want him to think about that cousin too much.

Instead she said, 'Oh, you know how it is, Rebecca's such a mouthful for a tiny baby, so I was Becky and it stuck.'

'Well, I've a good mind to call you Rebecca from now on. I like that name.'

'Please don't. I'd feel anything but myself and it would confuse the children. Becky's such a nice matey name for them to manage. Goodnight, Darroch. Here's hoping your predictions are wrong and it's only a flash flood.'

By the time she got into bed, however, the rain on the steep corrugated roof was deafening. Her bed was warm with its electric blanket. She was too sleepy even to read. Let tomorrow take care of itself.

The splendour of the world about them next morning had to be seen to be believed. Every plunging cliff and bluff beneath the eternal snow-line glittered with cascading water ... the air was filled with the singing. The sky was an inverted bowl of cobalt blue with never a cloud. Who could believe that so fierce a storm had put on a pyrotechnical display over the Cauldron last night? ... Or disbelieve it when they climbed to the Lookout and gazed out of the southern window far down the homestead hill to the river bank.

Was it the same river? That shallow bed must be six times its width now, brimming bank to bank with treacly-looking waters that tossed great willows about like corks, swirling evilly in innumerable eddies, scouring out huge chunks of gravel, bowling boulders along on the fringes, sucking and gurgling, a barrier to any communication by road.

'What about the men?' asked Rebecca. 'How far away are they by now? They won't get back tonight now, will they?'

'No, but as no river worthy of the name lies between here and No. One Hut, only gullies and creeks, by tomorrow they should be able to cross. The streams between aren't snow-fed and come only from minor hills, so the water soon drains away. Hope they're not short of provender. They'd kill a sheep anyway, and there are always tins of biscuits at the huts. Might even have a few potatoes left in the store there.'

She nodded as if remembering seeing how well the huts were stocked. 'But they'll be out of bread.'

'If they've flour left they'll make a damper. But we'll take plenty out of the deep-freeze tonight and if you can spare the time tomorrow, scones would go down well, and a couple of outsize puddings. They took plum duff up with them, easiest of all to stow on the pack-horses and re-heat—even to eat cold if need be—but if you could manage apple pies, there are plenty of packets of bought pastry in the freezer, a boon in an emergency. Like to give that a go?'

She'd have loved to offer to save the bought store and make the pastry, but dared not, it could land the real Becky in a hole if ever she was asked to repeat it. The phone rang. Rebecca still flinched at every ring, and longed to rush to answer, but it was the hospital ringing to say the operation was to be deferred till the following day.

Darroch was relieved. 'I didn't want to be beyond reach of the phone today, but I must get out to inspect the culverts this morning. I'll take a dekko at the ones nearest here first. I won't be in for lunch, so make the main meal for tonight. I'll pack bread and cheese and a flask in my saddle-bag. I dare not risk the culverts blocking with boulders—it could cause wash-outs. Especially the culverts near the track to Heronscrag.'

'I've got some soup at the back of the stove. Would you like a flask of it, or would it be a nuisance?'

'No, I'll take it. Thanks. I'll pack it. You'll have more than enough to do supervising the lessons and trying to run this. Don't keep on flying round at the rate you've been doing. I'm not expecting the impossible. You can't hope to run this, single-handed, as if it were a model home. Normally we've got Mrs McCosh at the housekeeping wheel and Sylvie and Ewan and family are at their own place. Cosh does a lot for Sylvie, of course, stocks up her cake deep-freeze once a week, to leave her free for the lessons, and at times when we're shearing or mustering, if no cook comes up with the gangs, she pitches in and we have to let the dusting and polishing go hang. You've proved your point. When you and Lennox get things straightened out, we'll work out a schedule.

'I mean when you're married. I reckon Cosh'd like a break from here ... that would help Sylvie, if she went across there. There's a three-roomed cottage over there, older than the house. Cosh could have that, and slacken her pace a bit. She could do the cleaning over there while Sylvie was busy with lessons. Becky, how would you feel about housekeeping for myself and Len till your own place was built? If you keep this up, I guess Aunt Davy'll buy in that land for Len—he'll have to repay of course, but at a very low interest if I know her—but it takes time to put a house up. Not ideal, I grant, having a household of three in the first year of married life, but we'd speed things up all we could, and I could see Len and you had a sitting-room of your own for your evenings. It's big enough.'

Rebecca said weakly, because she dared not commit Becky too much, 'We really can't decide anything yet, till Lennox cools off and comes back. We've got to realise that in that telegram he did say that he'd accepted B——' She stumbled, catching back the name, 'that he'd accepted my decision as final. So it all depends on how he feels when he returns. He—he may not even be pleased to find me here. It—it could be a shock to him.'

Darroch said, 'Becky, you've turned up trumps. I'd never have believed it myself, so I suppose I can't expect Lennox to, unless he has proof, but I'll do my best to convince him any way I can. Don't forget, girl, that just as you regretted what you'd done, and missed him by the time you got to Timaru, so he could be missing you now. Long days aboard a small boat in the vastness of the Pacific will give him lots of time for reflection. He'll expect you've gone home. Your mother may ring in a week or two with news of a letter for you from him. It could all blow over. Len should be in touch with me from Fiji. He said so in the wire. I'm going to wire the harbourmaster at Suva to ask Lennox Fordyce on the *Hibiscus* of Tauranga, New Zealand, to contact his brother by phone, reversing the charges, on arrival there, just to make sure.

'I'll tell Lennox how you regretted what you'd done, came back here to tell him so, found Sylvie rushed into hospital and pitched in here in great style, cooking and supervising lessons and all. That we'll make a mountain wife of you yet. How's that?'

Rebecca wished herself a thousand miles from here. She was being forced into making decisions for her cousin, for Lennox, without the faintest hope of being able to find out what either of them really wanted to do. It was then that she knew that as soon as possible, if Becky didn't contact her, she was going to have to tell this man in front of her that she was an impostor and a liar. If only, if only she could tell him right now and go. Someone in this Mackenzie country, so famed for hospitality, so famed for resourceful women, would come to the aid of a man left on his own with a huge sheep-station to run and three children, two on correspondence lessons!

But outside lay a river called Rubicon, a river that couldn't be crossed.

Some of her distress must have been reflected in her eyes. The man was standing close to her, a deep frown etched between his brows. He clutched her hand, said, 'Don't look like that, Rebecca Menteith—it's a tough proposition, aye, but we're used to tough propositions here. Not usually such emotional ones, but things that, at first facing, seemed incapable of being solved. Let's just play it along. Nothing can be done till we hear from Len. It'll take him time to get to Suva. When he does ring, if I'm not available, and you answer the phone, tell the operator when you expect me back and be very firm about no one else being allowed to take the call. Now, I'll get at that phone and get that wire away to Fiji.' Just as he went to relinquish her hand, he made a sudden surprise movement and clutched it again, raising it up between the two of them. Her left hand.

He gazed at it in surprise. 'You aren't wearing your ring! You didn't leave it with that note, I know. So it wasn't really formally broken off. You did leave a loophole by saying if he really loved you he'd get a farm nearer the coast and the main roads, so why aren't you wearing it now? Or have you left it off for the household chores?'

It was a loophole, but she dared not take it. She said, 'Until I hear from Lennox I don't feel justified in wearing it. Not after that wire.'

The brows came down, hiding the expression in those tawny eyes. She thought his lips compressed themselves into a straight line as if he held some strange emotion in check. Then he nodded. 'I can understand that, and admire you for it. Not to worry, Becky, I like you much better as you are since you came back to us. I can practically guarantee that Lennox will fall in love with you all over again.' His eyes glinted. 'I could almost fall for you myself.' It was said lightly and meant solely to cheer, but it cut Rebecca like a knife, because of this new knowledge of her feelings for him. She walked away.

She got the children settled, came back to the bedmaking which today, mindful of other chores, was more a matter of closing the beds up than of being very fussy. They made their own beds Saturdays and Sundays she knew by now, but not on schooldays as Mum liked them into the schoolroom by eight, so that in winter, or early spring as now, they could get out in the sunshine after dinner because the sun went down behind the Great Divide so soon after that.

She knew now that if Becky didn't ring before the river went down, she must confess this foolish prank and bear the brunt of his anger and scorn, because she could no longer take the responsibility of making decisions once she knew Lennox would be nearing Fiji. It had been one thing deciding on the spur of the moment to take her cousin's place and another continuing it without any idea where her cousin was.

And what *would* Becky say when she knew what Rebecca had done? Rebecca felt sick to her soul. All the times she'd felt exasperated with Becky's irresponsible behaviour through the years rose up in memory to jeer at her. The time Becky, forbidden by her father to run up any more bills in his name, had gone to the dress shop where Rebecca had an account, had gone in, supremely confident that the saleswoman would take her for Rebecca, and bought so lavishly it had taken her six months to pay her cousin back out of her allowance; the time a traffic offence notice was delivered to a bewildered Rebecca. She'd gone straight in to the transport office. They'd brought in the officer responsible. It had been a terrible moment when she'd realised it must have been Becky and that her cousin would be in very serious trouble indeed for showing Rebecca's licence.

The officer had gazed at her sternly, said, 'What's all this? Do you think I'm nutty or something? Of course it was you. I couldn't possibly not recognise you.' As impulsively as she'd acted the other day when Darroch had mistaken her for Becky, Rebecca had made an inspired bid to save her cousin, had burst out laughing and said, 'Oh, I know what's happened, and I don't blame you. I have a cousin who's as much like me as an identical twin. Our mothers *are* twins, our fathers brothers, and we actually share the same name, only she's usually called Becky to distinguish it. I did lend her my car last week. She was living with us when her parents were in Malaysia in a diplomatic post, and she got her licence in my car, so it would be in it. She doesn't have one of her own. It's just like my dear absent-minded cousin to fish in the glove-box and produce *my* licence. I'm lady editor of the *Chronicle*, and I was out of town that day at a women's conference at Wairakei. I flew to Rotorua. Can I bring her in to apologise to you?'

There had been a great deal of guffawing over it. Rebecca marched Becky in for them to compare the two girls later in the afternoon and the next week it was recorded by the department in the newspaper as one of the lighter moments of the Traffic Department's daily round.

But this time it was Rebecca who was the offender. It was like some lighthearted comedy on a T.V. programme, very funny to watch but hell to find yourself in, in real life. Though Rebecca knew she was now committed to confession, she felt a little better. She must wait till she could cross the Rubicon, though. It was unthinkable to go on living in this homestead, in the sort of atmosphere that would be created when she told all. Imagine the derision of Darroch Fordyce's shepherds, the irresistible temptation they'd have to spread the story, possibly even by phone if they were all cooped up here for long. She must still play it along.

Meanwhile ... the job in hand. She didn't know what had got into the children. The only time they were good was when the School was on the air. In the end Rebecca, nearly demented, left Nan writing an essay, took Robert out into the kitchen so she could oversee his Social Studies answers while she was getting on preparing stuff for tomorrow's bigger meals, and tried to stop Andrew from distracting his brother. Finally she picked him up, gave him three smart slaps on the bottom and said, 'That's just for starters. Any more of that behaviour, young man, and you'll get the sort of spanking your uncle would give you if he was here!'

Andrew was too astonished to cry, even. He said, without a tremble of the lip, 'I thought you were a softy!'

Rebecca had trouble keeping her face straight. 'Well, now you know I'm not perhaps you'll just sit on the floor and play with that Lego set. You don't often get the chance to have it to yourself, so make the most of it. I think you could make some jolly good buildings if only the others wouldn't try to help you.'

'Yes,' said Andrew solemnly, 'they always overshadow me.' Rebecca bit her lip.

Robert looked down on him in a most superior fashion, said jeeringly, 'I bet you thought that because she isn't family, she wasn't game to wallop you. But what a hope! I reckon she's like Uncle Darroch, when Mum 'n' Dad are round he leaves the walloping to them, but sails into us when he's in charge.

'Very true,' said Rebecca, 'but if that's just another bid to postpone answering those questions and getting on with your map, Robert, you'll be the next to have the vials of my wrath fall on your head. I want absolute silence for the next half-hour. I want to try a new cake. I'm not a very experienced cook, so if I leave anything out it'll flop and I won't be nice to live with!'

Silence reigned. It was heavenly. After playtime the children were so subdued and amenable, she allowed

Robert back in the schoolroom and seeing Andrew rubbing his eyes and twisting his absurd fair forelock, deemed rightly that he was sleepy, and by dint of allowing him a treasured book of Robert's as a special treat, he didn't object, and fell fast asleep in five minutes.

Her cake had another hour to go when the phone rang and she heard Becky's voice. What an anti-climax to hear Becky's voice sound so casual! 'Oh, hullo, Rebecca, you're still there, then? Fancy! I thought you'd have made up your mind in a couple of days that it was no place for your little cousin and you'd have hied off to your friends and gipsy caravan in Dunedin.'

It was unbelievable. Rebecca was silent from shock, then rallied and said, 'Becky ... I haven't even told them who I am!'

Becky's voice sharpened with surprise. 'Haven't told them who you are? Have you gone off your rocker, Rebecca? They'd know who you were the moment they saw you. Nobody else *could* look so much like me as my double cousin.'

Rebecca closed her eyes, said faintly, 'Becky, haven't you rung your mother? Don't you know?'

Becky laughed, 'Speak up, I can hardly hear you. I only just got that. The answer is, dear cousin, I haven't. Dad will be livid after the way he tried to persuade me not to become engaged to Lennox. He told me next time I dropped my bundle I could pick it up myself. So that's just what I'm doing, and very nicely too. But I left my skis up there so thought I'd get them to send them on. What did you say, Rebecca?'

'I said be quiet and listen to me, and if I suddenly appear to change the subject it's because the others will have come in. Now don't interrupt in case they do. *They all think I'm you, up here.* Darroch took it for granted when I arrived at his door that you'd had a change of heart and had come back. I hesitated about denying it too long and got caught up in a very awkward situation.

The day after you left, Sylvie got taken to Timaru Hospital for an operation for gallstones.

'Darroch thought you must have heard and had an attack of conscience and returned to look after the children. I saw it as the one chance of you reinstating yourself with this household and didn't tell him I wasn't you.'

Becky did interrupt then, naturally. 'But you'd never deceive Lennox into thinking you were me! He must be back there by now, surely?'

'He's not—and won't be for some time. This gives you a chance to get back here, wait in Fairlie and as soon as I can get down there on my own with this rental car, we can swap places and you can come up to Tekapo on the bus and they can collect you from there. That way they'll never suspect. This is a great chance for you to prove yourself; not only to win the respect of the people here—and they're fine folk—but your father's respect too.'

Becky burst into laughter, malicious laughter. 'Oh, Rebecca, you sound like a revival meeting ... come back to the fold, you sinner, and all will be forgiven. Not likely! Besides, Lennox'll be back long before I could get there. And then, dear cousin, the fat will really be in the fire and I don't want to be any part of it. You're one of the clear-minded, sincerity-at-all-costs types, I can't see you as an actress at all. One passionate embrace from Lennox and you'd give yourself away.'

Rebecca went cold with anger. 'Becky, you've gone too far this time, you're just abominably selfish! Yes, I know I oughtn't to have acted on impulse like that, but it was for your sake. I didn't want to come up here in the first place. I must be the most gullible fool in Christendom. Fancy trying to save your engagement ... I actually thought you'd regretted it, that you truly loved Lennox, but had just tried this on to get him to agree to a farm nearer civilisation. And you'd better know this, Lennox is so mad he hasn't turned up in Auckland ... he was go-

ing to chase you right up there ... but he diverted to
Tauranga, met up with that crew he wanted to join up
with months ago and is now somewhere between here
and Fiji. We *think* he'll be in touch with Craigievar from
Suva. So you'd better beat it back to Fairlie, leave a
message at the post office for me to say where you're
staying, and we'll swap places. It won't take you long
from Christchurch.'

She didn't like Becky's laugh. 'Well, for once, my dear,
so-efficient do-gooder of a cousin, you can't persuade
your mirror-image to do what you think she ought to do,
like apologising to a motor-cop for taking him in ...
I'm not in Christchurch and I'm not coming back to
Craigievar ever ... I'm in Wellington, with people I
knew overseas, *my* kind of people, not prigs like you.
People who know how to live and how to spend money.
As far as Craigievar exists I must have had a brainstorm. It's Lennox's own fault, he made it sound like a
little Switzerland, instead of a slave labour farm! I've
got other fish to fry now. I've got the chance of a Pacific
cruise ... paid for. As a companion to the sweetest
woman who doesn't like travelling alone.

'I'll show Lennox I'm not wilting on the bough and
pining for him. How delightful it would be if I banged
into him in Fiji! So you can do just what you like about
getting away from Craigievar. You'll have to put yourself
in the wrong for once, Rebecca, and tell the craggy Darroch you made a fool of him. Better get it over before
that ring from Fiji comes through ... or I wouldn't like
to be you. It serves them all right. Lennox has insulted
and humiliated me. I never want to see him again. I'll
leave you to tell Mother this, Rebecca,' she added. 'Let
her down lightly. She's not too bad. It's Dad I've no time
for. Wedded to a career that meant I had to be left behind
in my schooldays, with your family. From now on, I'm
living my own life,' and before Rebecca could implore
her to at least give her a number where Aunt Mirrie

could reach her daughter, Becky had hung up.

Rebecca went across to the table, dropped into a chair, leaning her hands on her head. She felt frozen, incapable of thought. The clock chiming half-past eleven finally brought her out of her paralysed state of mind. She must ring Aunt Mirrie now before the children erupted from the schoolroom. But she would have to water down the animosity, the sheer lack of feeling for parents who'd never found it easy to leave their darling only child.

This time luck wasn't with her. Uncle Alan answered the phone. By now Rebecca was used to blows of circumstances and wondered if Aunt Mirrie had taken ill. She hedged, played for time, asked how he was, how Aunt Mirrie was, and if he was busy at work just now, after his long convalescence.

'Mirrie's getting her hair done, that's all. Now, Rebecca, come to the point. By now your aunt has told me the lot as she jolly well should have done from the start. She watered it down to spare me, but I wormed the whole thing out of her. She was trying to save the situation between Becky and myself, but that won't work. Becky's got to face up to things sooner or later. I appreciate all Mirrie's done through the years, but having to be insulated from such things made me less than a father. It must have done, or my daughter wouldn't be such a selfish little devil, always involving other people in her affairs, and wriggling out from under with the least possible damage to herself.

'Lennox is far too good to be used like this. I thought it sounded unsuitable, but he was a fine young man and I thought that perhaps she really cared and it could be the making of her. I'm afraid she must have just fallen for him on the rebound. The only man she ever cared about was Kingsley Payne, and when he gave her up, because he couldn't stand her devious ways, it did something to her. Yet I always felt, because *he* didn't see her through rose-tinted spectacles, that he'd have been the one to make her toe the line. Now you're in a nasty position and Becky disappears into thin air. It was a damned silly thing to do, Rebecca ... you've got into the habit of pulling that girl of ours out of every boghole she's got herself into, but this time your quixotic impulsiveness over-ran your common sense.

'Before you tell me what you've rung up for I want to say this,' he went on. 'You must give up all idea of trying to smuggle Becky back into the homestead. Let her go her own way. Simply tell Darroch Fordyce what you did and why. He'll realise you'd never have planned it deliberately ... had he not taken you for Becky in the first place. Try to take it fairly lightly if you can, but if you can't, be abject and grovel. You've got that hired car ... I'll pay for that, by the way ... ford the river, get on to Dunedin and do the thing you've planned to do for so long and forget all about the Alan Menteith family. Let us dree our own weird, as Granny used to say. Just get over that river and go.'

He stopped for breath, as well he might, and Rebecca said, 'I can't. Not yet. The river is in flood. It will be at least a week before it goes down. I've got to stick it out till then. I just *couldn't* stay here once I confess. But as soon as it subsides, I'll go. I've just had a ring from Becky. She hung up without giving me a number for you people to ring. Said to tell you that she's staying with friends in Wellington just now, and is going to accompany some wealthy woman on a Pacific cruise. I hate telling you as bluntly as this, but I have to, in case anyone comes in. I——' her voice broke.

'Rebecca, don't be too upset,' said her uncle. 'I know you hate telling me this. What's more, I can guess you've toned it down a bit. Well, we must just let her go off on this cruise. Oh, sure, I could dive down to Wellington and go round the shipping offices to catch up with her, but I'll let her go off without a word. She'll turn up when she runs out of money. I'll let your mother and father

know what's happening. We'll run down and tell them—
you dare not put too many calls through from there. I'll
keep it light, Rebecca, so they don't get too frantic. Perhaps we could just moan together over our mad daugh-
ters as we used to do when you substituted for each other
as kids. As if it's just another scrape you and Becky will
laugh over when you're old and grey. Don't worry about
us, love. As soon as the river's down, get it off your chest.
They can't eat you. They won't want to spread it abroad.
They'll probably tell neighbours that Becky came back,
gave it a go, but finally decided high-country life wasn't
for her, so the engagement's off, a nine-days' wonder.
God bless you for trying to help, even if it didn't come
off.'

Rebecca choked. 'Oh, Uncle Alan, I do love you! I'm
going to confess I've always been a little afraid of your
logical mind, even though tremendously proud of you
and all you've accomplished in international relations,
but I feel nearer you at this moment than I've ever been.
I wish I could hug you. God bless you too, and love to
Mum and Dad and Aunt Mirrie.'

She sat down, limp as a kitten, on the nearest chair.
At that very moment Darroch Fordyce came in, carrying
his lunch. 'I'll have that here after all. I had to come back
for some tools.' He put it down on the table. 'Hey!
What's the matter? You going to faint?'

She tried to sound scornful. 'Of course not!' But even
to herself it sounded an extremely feeble effort and
seemed to come from far away. Every bone in her body
felt all of a sudden like spiral steel, not rigid, and she
began to slip off the chair.

She was caught, lifted up, with a hand under her neck
and another under her knees, and he strode across to the
kitchen couch with her. He laid her with her head hanging over the far end, and put the cretonne pillow under
her knees so that the blood would rush back to her brain.

Weak tears gathered in her eyes and slid down out of the corners.

He knelt beside her, holding her cold hands, and she felt his tremendous vitality flowing back into her. Her eyes began to focus properly again. 'I—I'm coming right.'

He smiled, his look of anxiety diminishing. 'Right, I'll ease you up, but gently. I won't put a pillow under your head yet, but I'll get you back on the squab.'

He took out a handkerchief, wiping the tears from where they were dribbling to the tops of her ears. 'You've been very spunky, but you've overdone it.'

She shook her head. 'No, I haven't really. It was quite sudden. First time in my life—what a horrible feeling, yet in a way it's a relief from tension. It won't happen again, I'm not in the habit of swooning.' She managed a laugh.

'Oh, you game little thing! You can even see the funny side of a swoon. That's what I mean by spunky.'

She turned her head a little to smile at him, then suddenly the smile went wobbly, because he had a strange look in his eyes. He was looking at her as if ... as if ... he was looking at her as she'd have liked him to look at her had she met him under different circumstances, not cluttered with Becky's former behaviour; had she been herself.

He said, 'Feel better now, girl?' and for a heavenly moment laid his cheek, still cold from outdoors, against hers.

At that very instant the door burst open and Robert and Nan erupted into the kitchen and stopped dead at this unusual sight.

Then Robert said with a deep indrawn breath and a reproving tone, 'What *are* you doing kissing Becky, Uncle Darroch? She's Uncle Lennox's girl!'

Fortunately both Darroch and Rebecca burst out laughing. To have looked guilty would have involved them further. Darroch recovered himself sufficiently to say, 'I'm not *kissing* her, you nit, I'm *cuddling* her. For comfort. Just as I'd cuddle Nan if she fell over. Becky fell off her chair in a faint. I think she's been doing far too much.' He grinned. 'Perhaps you two have been too much for her. Have you been playing up this morning?'

It was, had they but known, an idle remark, but it was evident immediately that the shot had gone home. Both children went absolutely crimson. 'Good life!' said their uncle. 'I think I've scored a bull's-eye. What *have* you been up to?'

Two pairs of eyes went to Rebecca's anxiously.

She sat up on one elbow. 'Good grief, Darroch, it would take more than a couple of quarrelling children to make me swoon! It was nothing to do with that. I had to separate them, that was all. They've been angels ever since. So has Andrew. He's asleep. I've put in a ginger-bread and a sultana cake since then—that proves they've behaved since. I was much too late to bed last night. I was reading that book over there and couldn't put it down.'

Robert picked it up. 'Any good for me? I can read thrillers now if they're not too violent, Mum says.'

Rebecca shook her head. 'Not a thriller. An historical novel about King Charles the First. When you're a bit older you——'

Robert interrupted, 'I thought you didn't like historical books. You and Uncle Lennox had a barney over it one day.'

Rebecca tried to think of some reason why she liked them now. Darroch saved her. He said in kindly fashion, 'Well, now that Len and Becky are going to be married, Becky wants to like the sort of books he likes. I daresay she'll even come round to doing crosswords too. Look at your mother. She had no interest in crosswords till she came up here and now she's such a fiend for them, your dad wishes he'd never introduced her to them. Anyway,

Becky was sure enjoying that book last night.' He laughed teasingly. 'She was even crying over it.'

Nan was looking at her appraisingly. 'How funny, anyway, that you didn't like that kind of book; you said yesterday that history was your favourite subject.'

'Well, I liked it as a school subject, but didn't like it much for leisure reading. But if I can get hold of more books like that, I'll become an addict.'

Darroch said with satisfaction, 'Ah, we're back to normal, you've got more colour in your cheeks now.' As well she might! she thought.

He got the kids setting the table. 'Just soup and toast. Andrew can have his later, I'm a great believer in letting sleeping dogs lie. Becky, stay right in your chair till we serve it up.' His voice dropped. '*Are* you feeling better, or was it Robert's surmise about the kissing that put the colour up? We can only pray he doesn't retail that to Lennox on his return.'

Rebecca thought drearily that when Lennox was back at Craigievar she could be anywhere in the South Island, living solitarily in a caravan, trying to make her living by freelance writing. It didn't seem half as entrancing a prospect as it had a month ago. In fact she seemed desolated ... because once someone like Darroch Fordyce came into your life, compelling, vital, dear, it would always be empty without him.

The alarm rang as she got up. Darroch looked startled. 'Who set that?'

'I did ... I'm such a novice at cooking I need reminding. I can't bear to burn cakes after the effort of making them. You said the men would come off the mountain with terrific appetites, so I'm stocking up.'

'Don't bend over the oven. I'll take them out.' The gingerbread was nicely cracked across the top, and the sultana cake was smooth and crisp. 'Well, for a novice you're doing very well. Not a failure yet.'

'Touch wood. That gingerbread is a bit high, it could sink.'

Nan got out the soup plates. 'Don't worry. A chocolate cake of Mum's did. She cut the middle out with a cup, iced the cut and the top and we thought it was a ring cake.'

'Perfidy of women,' said her uncle. 'But if it does sink we'll have the middle as a pudding, with a dollop of ice-cream and some of that left-over butterscotch sauce on it. I reckon that would taste Ritzy. Uncle Lennox is going to thank his lucky stars there was a crisis on here and that his Becky hurled herself into the breach and learned to cook.'

Rebecca thought if he mentioned Lennox once more she'd scream her head off.

CHAPTER FIVE

DARROCH had found the culverts very much in need of clearing. 'I'd have liked to get the ones on the far side of Nightcap Peak cleared after lunch, with help from you lot, but it's too far on foot and I don't think Becky would feel like tackling even old Ambling Andy after that swoon. You found him high enough as it was, the day we tried you out, didn't you? I think we'd better not have another attempt at riding till you feel more up to it.'

So her pretence at being frightened had been convincing. Now she could have wept with disappointment. She'd learned to ride as a child, had kept it up, and helped regularly at a friend's riding-school out of Auckland. If only they'd been teaching her to ski, no pretence would have been necessary. All she'd had in that line were two disastrous attempts on the nursery slopes of Ruapehu. Yet she'd always had a yen to live among mountains.

Nan said, 'We'd love to go, Uncle Darroch. You know Uncle Lennox took Becky up in front of him so she could get the feel of a horse moving under her without clinging for dear life round his neck ... I mean the horse's neck ... well, how about doing that again? Couldn't she go up in front of you? It'd be beaut fun this afternoon.'

Darroch cocked an eye in Rebecca's direction. 'It's entirely up to you. I know you still feel nervous, but all of a sudden you might get over that.'

She didn't hesitate. 'I'd like to try it again. Perhaps the success with the cooking has given me confidence.' What a hypocrite she was!

Andrew was humiliated by being told that as the terrain was steep he wasn't to ride his own small pony but go up in front of Robert, but was a little mollified when he found Becky was to be in front of Darroch. They packed some cookies and apples. The animals were saddled and Rebecca had to fumble a bit about mounting. The temptation to just swing up lithely was almost too much for her. Ambling Andy and Brownie looked wistful as the other horses trotted off.

Rebecca stopped wishing for a mount of her own. This had compensations, even though some of the ecstasy she felt with Darroch's arms about her, his chin on her hair, was mingled with pain because none of it was real; to him she was just his cousin's wayward, spoilt fiancée, suddenly turning up trumps, and when the day of reckoning came he wouldn't remember her even as that, but as a girl who'd made a sorry fool of him.

Meanwhile, Rebecca Menteith, enjoy what you've got. It will be something to remember. All your life you could recall the magic of this ... those silver-streaked cliffs where waterfall music echoed, birds such as she'd never noticed in Auckland calling, calling, not in golden song, but in strange wild cries, the very essence of loneliness.

She had plenty of colour now on the cheeks faintly dappled with freckles. She was in Graham of Menteith tartan slacks, with Becky's bulky-knit green jersey pulled over it, and a green and blue triangular scarf knotted at her throat. The hair lifted back in coppery streaks to blow across Darroch's cheeks and she turned her own cheek occasionally to hear more clearly what he was saying.

She leaned forward once to pat the chestnut neck, thrilling to the feel of the hide, the sense of muscle rippling under the warm skin. 'Good girl,' said Darroch. 'You're getting the feel of her. Suddenly you'll feel a rapport with your mount and wonder why you ever felt afraid. I don't ever look down on people for being afraid at first. It's different if you've been put in the saddle almost as soon as you could walk. I wasn't. I still remember the strange experience of having something with a mind of its own moving beneath me.

'We didn't start coming here for holidays till I was nearly twelve. We'd lived in the North Island before that and Mother was nervous about letting us come over the river in case we took ill and were cut off from medical aid. I felt Lennox was too impatient with you, Becky. *He* could ride soon after he could walk. I took him to task for hassling you, later, but he was dying for you to excel in front of us and he knew how necessary it is up here to be able to ride. There are times, even with a four-wheel-drive vehicle, when it's impossible to cross the Rubicon, but a horse can pick its way. As long as the rider doesn't look down, it's fine. Swirling waters make you dizzy.'

Rebecca thought dazedly, 'I'll think myself into *being* Becky yet! I feel I should thank him for tackling Lennox on *my* behalf. It was good of him when he so despised that same Becky.' She shook her head to rid herself of confusion. Why not just enjoy this delightful interlude? She gave herself up to the sheer joy of being within the circle of Darroch's arms.

There was a steady shoulder of hillside mounting up to the frowning crags of Nightcap Peak, with a rough track leading up. Below the rocks was a dell dented into the hillside where in all this bareness half a dozen larch trees had been planted.

'How idyllic!' cried Rebecca, and instinctively put a hand on Darroch's hairy forearm to restrain him. He reined in, looked over her shoulder, asked, 'What's idyllic? In particular?'

'Delightful that someone took the trouble and foresight to plant those trees just there ... not serving any purpose but to delight the eye. This whole place is like that. The stones in the hillside garden where someone has put pockets of soil so little creeping things may grow and put patches of colour there even in winter. The way the eye is led on and on through breaks in the shelter walls to other views. Just now it's a bare garden, just rocks and lichens and alpine plants, yet all the construction has a charm of its own. I'd love to write it up.' She stopped, appalled. What was she saying? That was the worst of being a journalist. You wanted to get everything down in colourful words for other eyes to read, for other imaginations to picture. You looked at life in terms of your newspaper. Old habits died hard.

He said, laughing, 'An author may have been born this very moment. I've heard of such things, some emotional experience triggering off some dormant desire to write. Perhaps it's in the family. Didn't you say your cousin is a reporter?'

'It could be, I suppose. Not a reporter, she edits a page for the *Chronicle*.'

'Then why not write this up ... aspects of life on a high-country sheep-station ... and send it to her? I expect they have features like that.'

'Yes, on Saturdays, but no, thanks.'

'Why not?'

'I think it could be embarrassing to have to turn down something a relation had written. It's easier to reject a stranger's stuff.'

'Well, why not give it a buck and send it to one of the magazines? Do it from the woman's angle. The hardships and rewards. You're just beginning to take to the high-country. This could give Len a thrill, yet, dammit, it has to be the time he decides to take to the high seas. He's going to get a shock when he gets back ... a very pleasant shock.'

A shock, yes, but *not* a pleasant one. Because neither Becky nor Rebecca would be here and Lennox's cousin was going to tell him a strange tale of someone taking Becky's place, making a fool of the boss of Craigievar and getting away with it for a short time.

Darroch said, his face an inch from hers, 'How odd, I'd not noticed before, you've got freckles. I've aye liked girls with freckles.'

She said, a little breathlessly, 'Well, thus far you've not been near enough to see them. Come summer they'll stand out more than I like them to. As a child I was covered with them.'

'Summer suns here are very fierce. Blinding too, striking back off snow, and the heat in the valleys can be stifling. You remind me of Christine Dean at Tekapo. She owned Heronscrag once. I don't think she and Henry were there when you went over. She's a sort of elderly cousin of Matt's. Your eyes remind me of hers. Must go with that colour hair, though hers is white now. Henry, who was parted from her for forty years before he married her, says her eyes are the colour of *paua* shells, mostly blue but not only blue, flecks of green in them in certain lights. Yours are too. I'd not noticed before.'

Of course he hadn't. It was only evident up close, and Becky's eyes were pure sapphire. She said, 'About those culverts ...'

He laughed, 'Aye, we're getting a bit personal, aren't we, lass? Here come the youngsters. We'll tie the horses under the trees, then slide down to the culverts. The kids like this job, it's the equivalent to building dams in streams.'

The far side of Nightcap Peak was ridged with miniature gullies leading down to the river far below, where the water tumbled and roared and leapt over huge boulders. Below them a track led right round the flooded edge of the river, and to preserve that track culverts were set underneath.

'Wouldn't it have been easier to ride round there?' she asked.

'Yes, but you'd miss the view. I feel in flood, it's at its most magnificent. Awesome, but splendid.'

It looked east and north. 'A great place to watch the

sunrise from,' said Darroch. Rebecca felt a pang that was almost physical. Some day this man would marry, bring a wife to the high-country, and make a ceremony, early in their marriage, of bringing her here to watch a sun rising over that spreading tussock plain, and touching these alpine heights with rose and coral, pearl and amber, amethyst and flame. But Rebecca Menteith would never see it. In less than a week she would be gone from sight of these mountains, from sound of torrent and cascade and the roar of avalanches. And they would be glad to forget her.

Robert gave a small boy's guffaw, nudged Nan, and said in what was meant to be a whisper, 'Changed a bit, hasn't she? Remember we heard her telling Uncle Len you couldn't live on views, that you needed to be able to see a strange face once in a while?'

'Shsh!' warned Nan, too late, turning red.

Robert's uncle said, 'Enough of that, young Robert. We all enjoy other company when we've been cooped up here too long. Becky's been a brick the way she's adjusted. It was as natural for her to feel homesick for city streets as it would be for you to feel homesick if you went off to boarding-school. We were pretty intolerant. But now she's shown she's got what it takes.'

Rebecca felt sick and ashamed for her own falsity.

They began scrambling down the sides, using the boulders as steps, sometimes sitting and sliding down the dry tussock. It was fun clearing the culverts. The storm had certainly jammed them with boulders large and small, and though there were plenty of chinks to let the water through as yet, before long the spaces could be choked with loosened tussocks and lichens and a great scouring-out of hillsides would result.

Once they moved a few boulders, the force of water increasing bowled others out of the way. They walked down to the brink of the river, keeping a firm hold on

Andrew. How hard it was to remember what this was like before the flood. Then it had been a limpid flow; now the silt had made it an evil consistency. It was fearsome, even malevolent-looking, which was fanciful, but it did seem to have a character and destructive force of its own.

'As it rises so quickly, Darroch, does it fall as quickly?'

'It can. That's logical, given the right sort of weather, but after a spectacular storm like that, snow-shelves are loosened and down it comes, melts, and keeps the river high. It could mean anything. We may be in touch with the outside world again in a couple of days, or cut off for considerably longer.

'Then, when the river does go down, we could get snow. The weather has a chance of levelling up the average and we nearly always find that we get our yearly quota of snow, and with so much less this winter, who knows?'

Rebecca said, 'I'm a ninny. I thought the snow would all be over.'

The children burst out laughing and all tried to talk at once. 'We've had snow on New Year's Day up here ... midsummer. Once we even had a white Christmas. We had all these people staying. They loved it, but we didn't. The lambs were so young. We lamb late.'

'But you'll love the snow too, Becky,' said Darroch, unaware he was striking a chill to her heart. 'Instead of having to go across to the Beaudonais ski-field like you did at the end of July when you first arrived, you'll be able to take off from our back door. What a help you'll be going round the sheep on skis!'

Rebecca closed her eyes for one terrified, dizzying moment. They'd think it was against the dazzle of the sun on the white splendid peaks. Take off from the back door on skis? She'd be revealed as a novice from her very first bumbling move forward. She must be out of here before any snowfall came. But if she wasn't, she'd just have to tumble down the Lookout stairs and pretend she'd sprained her ankle.

The Rubicon remained in flood for over a week, even though they had no more rain. As Darroch had predicted, loosened snow swelled the waters.

Rebecca knew a racing heart when the men first came in from the mountains. How was she to know what encounters, in a verbal sense, Becky might have had with them? It could have been, of course, Becky being snooty in some things, that she'd have felt she had so little in common with them, she'd not had any fellowship there. On the other hand, she liked masculine admiration. Heaven send she didn't get tripped up on something Becky had offered a decided opinion on.

It was evident that Darroch had met them and prepared them for a change. Must have told them they were to accept the fact that the cuckoo-in-the-nest had now put her shoulder to the wheel, and was turning out a blessing in disguise, thought Rebecca, mixing metaphors in an uncaring way remarkable in a newspaper columnist.

She wanted to laugh when their names were first mentioned, and had it not been she was supposed to have met them before, might have asked saucily was it a stated requirement for work on Craigievar that men of Scots ancestry were preferred? Really . . . Duncan Hay, Keith Farquharson, Lindsay Forbes. Perhaps it wasn't so remarkable; the Scots race were so often men of the mountains. Hadn't one pioneer, long ago, specified that he wanted Scots shepherds, used to their own hills and mountains, at Orari Gorge? Who was that? Oh, yes, Charles Tripp.

Duncan was a man in his fifties, dour-looking, but as kindly as they come. Keith was as redheaded as herself, son of a farmer beyond Fairlie but who intended, eventually, to try for a farm in the high-country when he got married, and Lindsay Forbes was at an agricultural college but was taking a year off from study to learn a bit more and gain practical experience.

Darroch had told Rebecca what he had intended to tell his men, and had met them outside to make sure. He was to say he'd persuaded his young cousin to take the chance of this Pacific trip when it was offered again, by phone, that with a full staff at Craigievar it was a good time to go, and that it was a pity that as soon as he'd left Sylvie had been rushed to hospital, but it had given Becky a chance to show what sort of stuff she was made of, and, by George, she'd certainly pulled her weight.

This bit of diplomacy, not to say deceit, comforted Rebecca somewhat. She'd regarded Darroch as the kind to have so much integrity that he'd tell the truth and shame the devil rather than prevaricate, so perhaps when it came to the time of confessing, he'd not regard her as such a despicable liar after all. He'd said to her, 'I don't want everyone to know that you and Lennox decided to split up because now you've settled down to life here so well, the less gossiped about the better.'

She was careful to wear Becky's jersey for their return. By now the children had stopped saying, 'Oh, I haven't seen that before,' or 'I didn't know you'd brought so many different clothes with you,' when she appeared in things they'd not seen before. She hoped the greetings from the children would single out the men for her. Her prayers were answered. The children were so fond of the men she knew in the first seconds.

Keith said, 'Hi, Becky ... good job you were here. Darroch's a cook only to be appreciated in emergencies, but this spread looks nothing like one of his. Good for you ... we redheads always come to the top when needed.'

'Like scum,' muttered Lindsay. 'I mean only Keith, not you, Becky. Oh, boy, are those apple pies? After all that duff, it's a lovely sight. We've got a couple of haunches of venison with us. We'll hang it tonight and cut it up for you for the deep freeze tomorrow. I guess the boss'll be able to tell you how to cook it if you've never done it before.'

Rebecca laughed. 'I might just be able to manage it. We had some given us in Auckland and I cut a recipe out of the paper and tried it and it was delicious.' True enough, and it could just as easily have happened to Becky.

Darroch looked delighted. It was evident he wanted his men to appreciate the change in his cousin's fiancée too. Not that it meant anything now. Becky wasn't coming back and all Rebecca had to do for her own sake was keep up the deception till she could reveal all and flee from their wrath, their justifiable wrath. Her self-respect was oozing away with every hour she spent in this magnificent mountain haunt. No good being scornful about the way Becky had shown up here, when her own behaviour was so open to criticism. The Fordyces would wash their hands of them and think the Menteiths were a very poor lot and it was better to be rid of them than have Lennox marry into a family like that. She must serve this family as best she could till that ghastly river subsided and she could ask them to make arrangements to get some responsible woman in to look after the children.

Showers were the order of the day for the men. They had a couple in their own quarters, but there were three showers adjacent to the schoolroom and Darroch brought them up here today. 'It's warmer, and anyway, I'll have Duncan sleep up at the house till Sylvie gets back, or Ewan. She's going to stay with the Winmores when she's discharged. The doctor said, according to Sylvie, "We don't like post-operative cases marooned in a Godforsaken spot like that." You can understand it.'

Before she thought Rebecca said indignantly, 'I can understand him wanting her nearer expert attention, but he'd no right to call it Godforsaken!'

Four faces boggled at her, then Keith said, 'Well, for crying out loud, you sure have changed! You called it the most uncivilised spot in New Zealand when you first came up here. Now you're up in arms because a city wallah calls it Godforsaken!'

She reddened uncomfortably, which made them look at her with interest. She said hesitantly, 'Well, you know how it is. It's not civilised if you mean by that buses passing the door and airports close at hand and theatres and schools, but it's far too beautiful to be forsaken by its Creator. I hate that term.'

Lindsay said admiringly, 'I'll go along with that. Gosh, you're a funny girl. You couldn't stand the place when you first came here and now you're up in its defence.'

The dour-looking Duncan put his oar in. 'Leave the lassie alone. I've aye liked people who can change and admit it. People who never change their minds about places or folks are weak, not strong. You just needed to be needed, didn't you, lass? Mebbe you're a loner like me, like to be in charge. And if those pies are in the nature of an olive-branch, we'll grasp it with both hands. I'm for getting cleaned up and ready to do justice to that meal. What's for first course?'

'Soup, then roast topside.'

Lindsay said, 'Well, we couldn't, I suppose, expect Yorkshire pudding with it? That'd be too much to expect. Forget I asked.'

Darroch grinned. 'You're in luck, but the praise is not all hers. She'd never made one before but would like to give it a go and if it was a flop—well, there was always the pig's bucket. So I said I'd help her. I beat the eggs. But we made it too darned soon, so go for your lives. It seems to be all right sitting under that cloth on the rack, but we've a feeling it's so puffed up it might sink into a soggy mass any moment.'

It didn't, so the cooks got puffed up instead. Sheep

talk lost Rebecca at the table, but she wasn't worried because she couldn't imagine Becky absorbing any of that or being even faintly interested, so she and the children kept up an undercover conversation while the men talked and argued. She liked the way Darroch, while still remaining the boss, deferred to Duncan Hay's long experience.

In a pause Rebecca said, 'How extraordinary, all of you come—in a clan sense—from the same area, Fordyce, Hay, Farquharson, Forbes. Was there a general migration from the east coast of Scotland to these parts?'

Keith seemed as impulsively spoken as herself. He didn't hide his astonishment. 'Are you even getting interested in the history of the place now? How come you know so much about us when in the first place you told us you'd not even bothered to visit where the Menteiths came from when you were in Scotland?'

Dangerous ground ... Rebecca, who'd have loved to visit the territory of the Menteiths, Grahams, Stewarts, had never been to Scotland. The whole company was looking at her. Young Robert saved the day. 'Oh, she got interested in that book about clans and tartans in the schoolroom. It's yours, isn't it, Uncle? She was looking in it while we were doing essays.'

He added, glad to have the grown-ups' undivided attention, 'She says it's good to know these things, that it's part of our ejucation. Which sounds pretty funny to me. Says we'll never know when we mightn't appear on a quiz programme so the more general knowledge we—um—absorb the better. Gee, I wouldn't half like to win one of those beaut prizes ... like the Honda bike. Uncle, when d'you think I'll be allowed to get a trail-bike for round the station? I wouldn't need a licence for just getting round the farm.'

His uncle grinned. 'Nobody'll get a trail-bike before they're old enough to go on the roads. Your mother'd never have another moment's peace with you careering

If you were in their place what would you do?

Jeanette...

Though she has survived a heart-wrenching tragedy, is there more unhappiness in store for Jeanette? She is hopelessly in love with a man who is inaccessible to her. Her story will come alive in the pages of "Beyond the Sweet Waters" by Anne Hampson.

Juliet...

Rather than let her father choose her husband, she ran...ran into the life of the haughty duke and his intriguing household on a Caribbean island. It's an intimate story that will stir you as you read "The Arrogant Duke" by Anne Mather.

Laurel...

There was no turning back for Laurel. She was playing out a charade with the arrogant plantation owner, and the stakes were "love". It's all part of a thrilling romantic adventure called "Teachers Must Learn" by Nerina Hilliard.

Fern...

She tried to escape to a new life...a new world...now she was faced with a loveless marriage of convenience. How long could she wait for the love she so strongly craved to come to her...Live with Fern...love with Fern...in the exciting "Cap Flamingo" by Violet Winspear.

Jeanette, Juliet, Laurel, Fern...these are some of the memorable people who come alive in the pages of Harlequin Romance novels. And now, without leaving your home, you can share their most intimate moments!

It's the easiest and most convenient way to get every one of the exciting Harlequin Romance novels! And now, with a home subscription plan you won't miss *any* of these true-to-life stories, and you don't even have to go out looking for them.

You pay nothing extra for this convenience, there are no additional charges ...and you don't even pay for postage!

Fill out and send us the handy coupon now, and we'll send you 4 exciting Harlequin Romance novels absolutely FREE!

Get your
Harlequin Romance
Home Subscription NOW!

- Never miss a title! ● Get them first—
  straight from the presses! ● No additional
  costs for home delivery!
- These first 4 novels are yours—FREE!

◀ **For exciting details,
see special offer inside.**

Printed in U.S.A.

Canada Post
021
Postes Canada

over these rough mountain tracks. High-country men like you and me do our rounds on hobnailed boots, Robert. Same as we don't muster on horseback, but on foot. And that's it.'

Robert subsided.

Duncan's grizzled face creased into a smile. 'You'll wonder who's educating who, I shouldn't wonder. You'll find yoursel' getting interested in all sorts of things you never thocht of, lass. We've all had to lend a hand in the schoolroom at times, so we well ken what you're putting up with. Like the cooking it's fair wonderful what you can discover you can do when you have to. Reminds me of poor Gwillym Richards when he delivered his wife's twins. They came ower early and he panicked and Verona had to do some straight talking to him to pull himself together. Said if a high-country shepherd couldn't deliver his own bairn who could? To hear him now you'd think he never turned a hair! But no doubt Verona would tell you the day you were there?'

She took a chance. 'Yes, but just mentioned it in passing.' She filed that away in memory, in case the Richards, who owned a small plane, flew down before that river subsided. However, the next remark left her feeling weak. It came from Lindsay. 'You'll be in demand once you marry Lennox. Perhaps before. When we went to Dragonshill and they discovered you could speak French and German to the manner born, Penny and Hilary were so delighted they said to me on the quiet that they're going to ask you to take classes in those languages for the Dragonshill brood. They feel now Madame Beaudonais is gone those two languages could fall into disuse, and Francis and Charles haven't time to teach the children. They're fluent, of course, because their father was German, Carl Schmidt. They'd like it retained so that a vocal link will always be possible when the children go off to visit French and German cousins. It sounds good to me. It would give you an outside interest.'

He looked at the empty plates on the table. 'You've already proved you can rise to the situation, but you won't want your nose always to the domestic grindstone and I reckon you'd enjoy that. You've lived such a cosmopolitan life you'll need more than the run-of-the-mill grind here.' He stopped, grinned, said, 'Just listen to me, will you? It comes from taking psychology for a year at Otago University before I went to Lincoln. I think I know all the answers. But you'd take it on and enjoy it, wouldn't you?

Rebecca felt reckless. Her French was very much the schoolroom type, though she could read it reasonably well, but holding a conversation in it would be very halting ... as for German, she hadn't studied it at all. Becky, of course, had learned it in the best way possible, after her preliminary studies in it, living in those countries with her parents after she left school. But she herself would be out of here soon. 'It's an idea, Lindsay. Might as well use what talents I have. Because my culinary ones are still at the experimental stage. It's more by good luck than anything that I produce a good meal.'

'And guts,' said Keith. 'It takes guts to take on anything unfamiliar.'

Taking it all round, Rebecca went to bed feeling they'd certainly accepted her as Becky, but there were pitfalls in plenty ahead. The Richards could fly in a party from other homesteads any time they took it into their heads. God forbid they should bring in the Beaudonais-Smiths, or Joanna Greenwood for that matter. Darroch had mentioned once that she was quite a linguist. They could bowl her out any time if, for fun, they suddenly addressed her in French or German.

Perhaps she ought to pray for snow, to put landing on the airstrip out of the question. Snow? But *then* they'd expect her to use Becky's skis. She was in a cleft stick. Oh, please, God, I've been foolish, and I've lied and lied, but let that river go down and go down quickly, even if means I'll never see Darroch again and even if he does remember me it will be only as a member of a family they saved Lennox from marrying into. And thanks, God, that Lennox is in the Pacific and incommunicado and that Aunt Davina is too. Oh, river of Rubicon, subside, subside! Her mind scurried round all that Becky had said. One thing still puzzled her. Why had Becky said Lennox had insulted and humiliated her? Wasn't the boot on the other foot? After all, *she* had jilted *him*. Or at least laid down some impossible condition. But finally, because the day had been full of shock and hard work, and riding, in the rare mountain air, she slept the sleep of the exhausted.

From then on she seemed to live either on the heights or the depths ... not being able to discipline herself to stop enjoying Darroch's companionship, and the good comradeliness of the men, and the unexpected sweetness of the children as they came to love and trust her, even if that brought its own pangs, but also having the nerve strain of watching every word, looking for pitfalls, pretending to be a novice at things her mother had brought her up to do all her life.

She felt she enjoyed their T.V. watching most of all, when conversation ceased to be a trap and peace and tranquillity descended upon their household. She'd not thought to find television up here, but the few runholders in the area had decided it was worth clubbing together the huge sum necessary to be able to offer their men one of the amenities of down-country employment.

So when the children were tucked down they watched the news, more grateful for it than ever, now the river barred them from riding over for mail and papers; serials, plays, excellent New Zealand documentaries. She busied herself with the huge darning basket then because this terrain was hard on the feet. She felt that when she left here, if freelancing in a caravan palled, she ought to try the stage because playing this role had made her feel a first-rate actress had been lost in her!

It got a little easier when the men accepted that this one-time scatty girl of Lennox's was adapting to the life up here in an admirable way. They began taking it for granted she'd turn up in the woolshed, with the children; at the sheep and cattle-pens outside, even invited her down when any aspect of farming she'd not seen before was on. 'You're going to be another Joanna Greenwood,' Darroch told her, finding her helping them draft, her face covered with dust, hair wild, clothes filthy. 'And no finer praise could be bestowed. Even Duncan says you're no sae bad, and if you know any Scots folk, you'll realise you've won him over completely. Half of it, mind, is your newly-acquired interest in Scottish history. Pity Lennox hadn't been here to see this transformation. If only we had an address I could send an airmail to tell him, but I'll sing your praises when he rings me, as I've requested via the harbourmaster.'

She went cold with dread. 'Darroch, when he rings don't say anything to him. Don't even tell him I'm here. Don't ask me to explain this ... I have my reasons ... but I feel I must speak to him myself, in private. If he rings, would you just say "There's someone here who wants to speak to you," and call me to the phone and leave me?'

(Then she'd confess to Lennox that she'd tried to save the situation for him but hadn't because Becky wasn't coming back and that as soon as she could she was going to confess all and disappear from their ken for ever more.)

Darroch looked down on her, said gently, 'You're very worried about your next encounter with Len, aren't you? I don't blame you. It's always easier to get something over quickly and if he hadn't gone off like this, he'd have been here to find you game enough to give it another go, and what's more, doing a splendid job. But don't worry, girl, he'll be missing you as much as you're missing him; that's half way to a reconciliation.'

She nodded, having to accept that, having to keep playing it along. He reached out and took her hands. 'Your hands are cold. You really are scared of how Len will take it. Don't be. It will come out right. I'll make it right for you ... with him. You're over your homesickness now—that's what made you so edgy with each other. I'd never seen Len like that before. It will be so different now. You won't keep on scrapping with each other now. That's what got at us all, lack of harmony. But that's behind you. We ought to have realised what an impact this sort of country would have on someone who's lived a life like you have. I was the one who ought to have known, from my own trip overseas. And it was all so far from normal, Cosh being away, and Sylvie over here with the children. It added up to too many personalities for you to relate to.'

The men had cleared off, either because they had to, or had sensed there was some straight talking going on. Anyway, they were all in the woolshed now.

Darroch continued, 'You've been a brick. You must be tired, yet you do so many chores you needn't do. It's been tough for you, coping with this, with your future husband out' on the great blue sea somewhere, and the flaming river still up so we're all cooped up here together with no diversions. But some day all will be back to normal. Look, when Len rings, I'll try to get him to fly back here pronto. Oh, I'll let you speak to him first, but don't let him go till I get back on the line to do my persuading.'

Rebecca didn't look up, didn't know what to say. He put a finger under her chin and forced her to look up at him. 'How's that?'

She caught her lower lip between her teeth. The urge to tell him all was almost too much for her. If she could have done it and gone over the Rubicon, she would have done it there and then. Although ... she'd have to give Darroch time to get someone in here to look after the children. They couldn't have their lives disrupted any more. There must be someone to keep an eye on Andrew in this terrain that wasn't the safest for an adventurous four-year-old. Someone to keep them looked after when spring chills could attack, someone to set their correspondence lessons, keep them up to date, and happy. That last was the most important of all.

She shook a little with the intensity of her feelings, knowing she must carry on for a little while yet for the comfort and well-being of this little family in all this immensity of mountain, rivers, and gorges.

Darroch's face held only tenderness and understanding. How could she ever have thought him harsh and forbidding, the autocratic cousin of Becky's picturing, who'd made a bad situation worse for an ill-assorted engaged couple?

He let go of her chin and took her hand again. 'Becky, you're afraid Lennox *is* taking this break as final, aren't you?'

She found herself nodding. That could account for her distress. She wished ... at least she thought she wished he'd let go of her hands. His nearness was disturbing.

Suddenly Darroch laughed. 'He won't, you know. He'd be a fool if he did, *now*. But if he does, Becky, by all that's holy, I'll snap you up myself. The way you've been, full of grit, trying anything and everything, from Yorkshire pudding to eye-clipping sheep and learning to ride, you'd make such a splendid high-country wife, I'm damned if I'd let you go.'

He let her hands go suddenly, said, 'Just as well the men are in the shed and the three kids way over there. If young Robert and Nan spot us like this again, I don't know what they'd say, but chin up, Becky. I'm quite sure everything will turn out for the best.' He strode off to the shed. Becky went across to where the children were building a dam in a very shallow stream. Her vision was blurred.

It had been just a laughing, meant-to-cheer-her-up statement and he'd never know the stab it had given her. If only she'd met him under different circumstances! As just Becky's cousin, and guest! If they had met like that and been drawn to each other as now, might they have come to love each other? To marry? Oh, there were too many ifs. She'd blotted her copybook badly. Even if he were the most forgiving man on earth, and *didn't* resent being made such a fool of, she could never stay here. Becky had made the break with Lennox complete. Darroch had Lennox living in his house with him. He couldn't, wouldn't do that to his young cousin ... marry the exact physical counterpart of the girl Lennox had loved, and who had jilted him. Lennox must have been cut to the heart to desert his post here and take off on a cruise. It was an unthinkable situation.

She must stop casting about in her mind for some tiny chink of hope. Soon they would stop having these sudden daily downpours interspersed in the hours of dry, glorious alpine sunshine, and that river would go down. She'd try to take it as calmly as possible, ask Darroch to get this Meg King who seemed to be a relation of the folk who farmed Pukewhetu, nearer Tekapo, to come to keep house till either Sylvie or Cosh got back. Sylvie was doing exceptionally well. Darroch rang every day.

She had an idea Darroch would be so furious, he'd arrange everything like lightning, to get her out of the house and have the whole ridiculous episode finished with.

And life would never be the same again for one Rebecca Menteith. She would carry on, because one had to, no matter what befell one in the strange region of the emotions.

Always she would carry with her an unappeased long-

ing for this huge triangular holding bounded by two
rivers and the backbone of the giant mountains of the
Great Divide. The banded dottrells would build their
nests in the shingle of the river beds, the white herons
would sometimes be seen, grace itself in their snowy,
curving flight against the cerulean skies, lizards would
haunt the sun-warmed stones and tussocks, gulls would
utter their lonely keening, coming in over the high tops
from the West Coast, sunset and sunrise would make
a glory of the skies and snows, but she would never see
them again.

'Becky,' called Andrew as she neared them, 'do come
and help us build a really big dam. It's great fun!' She
got down on her knees and began. Just carry on with the
little things, Rebecca, till the day you say goodbye to
them all.

CHAPTER SIX

THE days passed in their usual manner. The river subsided, then with more rain, lapped nearly as high as before. Each day she grew more attached. Even the thought of leaving the cats gave her twinges at times. Mehitabel grew so fond of Rebecca she'd sleep on her bed if she wasn't chivvied off, Jumping Jehosaphat was always in trouble; he headed for mischief as naturally as Andrew did. Rebecca chronicled his doings in her diary. She was an inveterate diary-keeper, though no day's page was ever long enough, so it was more like a journal. Her parents would enjoy reading it when all this was over. Her inner thoughts and fears and hopes were never recorded. Zachariah took his lordly way undisturbed by any of the pranks the other two got up to.

The dogs burst into a chorus of barking as soon as she appeared at the back door, hoping more of her generous titbits were to come their way; the horses whinnied and came to the fence. Darroch was surprised at the aptitude she now displayed in riding. That made things a little easier when they took their long treks out over the territory, though she was careful not to appear too proficient and confident. She had another reason too ... she liked to be helped up into the saddle by Darroch. Liked to be helped down too. Nan observed shrewdly one day, 'Isn't it about time she did that herself, Uncle Darroch? She's past the learner stage now.'

He said, very quickly, his hands slipping up from her wrists to her shoulders as if to steady her, 'I'm taking extra precautions ... if the cook breaks a leg we're sunk.' Rebecca rather despised herself for enjoying these physical contacts so much, for seeking them, even. It would only make it harder to leave. Sometimes at night they danced in the big side porch, that was like a miniature ballroom, with a beautifully polished floor, and a well-tuned piano. Even Duncan was a good dancer and saw that he got his turn. The memory of the dances she had with Darroch would stay with her for ever, she knew.

Most of the time, however, she was engaged with schoolroom or kitchen chores. She'd left the children busy on a project and was grating carrots for the soup when the phone rang. She was almost developing a complex about that phone, each ring giving her an apprehensive feeling that this might spell out her unmasking. It could be Becky, not yet on board the cruise ship, thoughtlessly ... or maliciously ... ringing. It might be Lennox, having reached Fiji much earlier than they thought possible, or Aunt Mirrie. It could even be her own parents, demanding she finish at Craigievar ... even though (oddly enough) they had great confidence in their daughter. Or had, till now!

This was none of those, but didn't exactly add to her peace of mind. An English voice, charming, gay. 'It's Joanna Greenwood here. I ought to have rung long since to find out how you were faring with these rivers up, but the weather's been so bad, since that spectacular storm, I wanted to wait till we had a chance to make plans. However, I was speaking to Darroch on the phone yesterday and he was telling me you'd been a tower of strength to them with Sylvie away.

'But I've just had a marvellous idea. Verona rang from Four Peaks to say the forecast for tomorrow is good and she was going to get Gwillym to fly her over here for a change. I told her how you'd pitched in in this emergency, and we've kidded Gwill to fly us all in to your place. It would give the children a jolly good Saturday holiday, poor lambs. My two have been fighting cat and dog here, and it does them good to have a few strangers thrown into the arena. Don't worry about the midday meal, Verona and I would bring it all with us. Can't descend upon anyone without all sharing in the meal prep. Don't feel it's because you're a novice at the game, we always do it this way. It won't be a long visit. It's only a weather-permitting one anyway, it so soon clouds over in the mountains, but it'll do us all good.'

Rebecca dared not appear anything but delighted, though she hoped she made no blueys not knowing what they'd talked about with her cousin on other meetings. She had a feeling Darroch would expect her to show her improved lore in the matter of housekeeping, so she said, 'Look, you can bring the desserts if you like, but I'm gradually becoming a medium sort of cook, so I'll see to the main course. And if we get spoofed by the weather, I'll deep-freeze my casseroles and have them next time you come. I tried out a rather snazzy venison dish the other night, so I'll do it again. Better than trying another new one on unsuspecting visitors.'

'Good for you! You know, of course, from your visit up here with Len, that when I got stranded up here I couldn't as much as boil an egg, so you don't need to worry on my account. Becky, we'll have people all round us tomorrow, so I'll just say now, in private, I think it was wonderful of you to let Lennox go off on that trip he's always wanted to take, leaving you here. I'd not have blamed you had you gone home to your mother while he was away, so it seems to me you've got what it takes for a high-country wife. What a blessing you were there when Sylvie was rushed off.'

Oh dear, would the children give her away tomorrow? They knew she'd been down in Timaru when their mother was taken away. She didn't think they knew Becky had walked out on Lennox. Had probably been told Becky had gone off to town with the truck-driver when he offered to take her, for a few days' shopping. She'd have to hope and pray.

She managed to sound delighted when Darroch and his men came in for lunch. They were so glad for her she felt more of a cheat than ever. If only she'd been herself, she thought despairingly, say the governess up here, how she would have welcomed this chance of shared hospitality and neighbourliness. As it was, she'd have to be very careful to sort out Matthew from Gwillym, Verona from Joanna. Mercifully the children saved her from that nerve strain.

Robert said enthusiastically to his uncle, 'I'll be able to show Dai and Rhys those photos we took at their place on the toboggans. Becky, would you like to look at them? Uncle Matt and Aunt Jo and their kids were there that day too.'

'I certainly would,' said Rebecca warmly.

The snaps, in colour, were glorious and it was fortunate Rebecca was able to say, 'Goodness, they're so muffled up I can't tell one from the other. Is that Joanna or Verona?'

Therefore the two older children pitched in with names. Verona was taller and her hair was more chestnut than red. Joanna's was even brighter than Rebecca's. Rebecca began to relax. She memorised the children's names. The Richards twins were so alike no one would think it odd if she mixed them up and the Greenwood children were younger, Rosamond four, and fair like her father, and Christopher six and very dark.

Darroch got them all regimented. 'It's no good you children thinking you can have all the fun of the fair and no chores. This is a big effort for Becky. I'm going to help her cube the venison tonight, late, when it's half thawed, but right now, you two are going to peel potatoes and put them into water with salt. What other vegies, Becky?'

'I'm going to do venison casseroles with raisins and thickening, nothing else, and sprinkle them just before serving with ground almonds and chopped glacé cherries same as I did the other night. I've no idea of the likes and dislikes of the Greenwood and Richards children, but I find decorations like that make even the prosaic dishes go down. So they can just get their vegetables in the soup. I haven't got enough frozen, but there's mutton stock and chicken stock in plenty in the freezer, so I'll have piles and piles of carrots, onions and leeks chopped.'

'The men can do those,' said Darroch, laughing at their faces, 'while I assist you with some cookies. I'll do the beating, chop nuts and so on.'

The men looked at him sourly. 'So we're the mugs who get the watery eyes from the onions; there's something in being the boss. You can nibble nuts, too.'

'If he's going to nibble,' said Rebecca, 'he can jolly well whistle while he works. That's what my mother used to make us do when we shelled peas.'

'Us?' said Darroch. 'I thought you were an only.'

'I mean my cousin and her brother. My parents sometimes got home for Christmas and took a seaside cottage and had us all there.' Phew! The slightest remark could trip you!

They all worked well and apart from burning some ginger crisps and dropping an egg on the floor, they were well rewarded.

Lindsay said, 'Becky, can I invite my girl-friend up here while you're managing? She's in an office in Christchurch. I didn't meet her till I went to Lincoln. She's obviously terrified of getting seriously involved with me in case she couldn't take the life. I'm hoping to get a job on a place like this, with married quarters. She's been writing to ask me how Len's fiancée is taking it and it's put me on the spot a bit. I've admitted—till now—that you were finding it hard going, didn't dare do anything else, but I'd love her to see you now. How about it? Could you manage a visitor when the river goes down? I reckon she could get a week off.'

Rebecca had to hedge. 'It's vastly complicated, Lin, because I just may have to go home for a bit before Lennox gets back. Mother rang the other day. We've some overseas friends coming out here and she'd like me to be home when they're entertaining them. And anyway, it's not my house, it's Darroch's.' She turned to him, 'You spoke about this Meg King—I gather she helps at Pukewhetu. Could they spare her to come to look after the household for a bit if I have to leave? Even if Sylvie came home soon, she won't be allowed to overdo things at first. Would Meg do it?'

She realised they were all looking at her in amazement. What had she said amiss? She faltered, 'You—you think Queenie King couldn't spare her niece? That it's not fair to ask?'

Darroch was looking at her, she was sure, as if he didn't like her very much. Why?

He finally said slowly, 'Of course she helps at Pukewhetu—been there more than a year. Certainly Queenie would spare her in an emergency ... to any other house in the Mackenzie Country, but we could hardly expect her to come to housekeep here instead of you.'

Rebecca felt her cheeks grow hot. 'You—you think it would be an imposition?'

He was short, said, 'I do. We won't discuss it now.' His gaze flickered to the children. Fortunately they were quarrelling. He said, 'Break it up, you two. The red peeler's no better than the orange one. Just get on with it. Till now you've not cared which colour you had. You're almost finished and you've been very good, so don't spoil things now.'

The two men who slept down at the quarters took a few samples of the cookies and went off to make their own snack. Duncan had his with Rebecca and Darroch, said goodnight and went off to his room.

Rebecca knew Darroch was going to say something to her. He seemed ill at ease—probably didn't want to upset her just when a horde of visitors was to descend upon them. Finally she said, 'What is it, Darroch?' and met his gaze fairly and squarely.

His brows were down, his face grim. 'You know there's

something, don't you?'

'Yes. I've put a foot wrong and don't know how, so you'd just better tell me. I won't get offended or sulky. Just fire a broadside. I'd rather that than feel an atmosphere like this.'

'Right. Surely you must realise why you can't ask Meg to do you a favour?'

She was stumped. She was supposed to know Meg, evidently, and why she wouldn't want to come to Craigievar. She took a deep breath, braced herself mentally, said, 'You'd better cross the t's and dot the i's, Darroch. I must be a bit dim, but for the life of me I can't seem to click.'

'Can't seem to click? That's coming it a bit thick. Surely to goodness it was evident to you that till you came on the scene we all thought Meg and Lennox would eventually make a match of it? It hadn't come to either of them being committed, or Lennox would never have brought you here as suddenly as he did. I mean there was no formal engagement to be broken, but we all thought and so did Meg——'

Rebecca said, 'I *didn't* know, or I wouldn't have suggested you ask her here to help out if I go home.'

'I find that extremely hard to credit. That was what I liked least about you before ... the way you treated Meg when you met her.'

Rebecca closed her eyes for a moment's respite, then said, 'What way did you think I treated her?'

'You made a petty triumph out of it. And there was nothing any of us could do to take the sting out of it for Meg. Oh, you've changed. We've had to admire the way you've pitched in here. I feel the mountains themselves have done something to you—very few people can stay petty in the shadow of these giants. But you're not going to use Meg to serve your interests, that's for sure. In actual fact, the way you spoke to Meg that day was, in my opinion, the first crack in your relationship with Lennox.'

Rebecca's head was whirling. Finally she said, in deep abasement, 'I'm sorry. I realise now that that was ... shabby. I can't say any more than that I'd not have suggested her coming here just now, had I known it had gone so deep with her. I—can't do anything about it, Darroch, can't wipe it out. So can we just leave it? Oh, before long there are all sorts of things I *must* explain to you. I've faced up to the fact that it will be better for everyone if I accept the fact that Lennox is through with me. It's got to be that way. Let's get this visit over, it won't be for long. Then you could contact Mrs McCosh and get her to come back sooner from Australia, to be with Sylvie. I'll have to get away from here before too long.'

He stood considering that, then, 'It will take some thinking out. I don't dare precipitate anything. It's for you and Lennox to decide. Let's leave it at that. Can you manage to keep playing it along?'

She gave that instinctive squaring of the shoulders. 'I can. Can you?'

'I can,' he said. 'And so goodnight.' They both went to bed.

Darroch was up long before Rebecca the next morning. She'd have liked a good start too, but didn't go out. The less time she spent alone with him the better for her peace of mind. Perhaps for his too. Naturally he'd feel he couldn't be responsible for her leaving Craigievar before his cousin came back, but he needn't worry. She had to go, but not for the reasons he thought. He'd know her then for a liar and a cheat. He'd be so furious at the deception, even if she'd done it in a sentimentally weak moment, that he'd probably not even take it in at first telling.

She wouldn't shower this morning, she'd had one last

night, and there was a wash-basin in this room. She slipped into her Graham of Menteith trews, pulled a green sweater over her head, decided to leave her hair loose as Becky always did, though lately, working round, she'd been tying it back, but to the visitors she wanted to appear exactly as Becky had. Well, it might be easier to have other people in the house today.

She didn't think it had rained last night, so perhaps the river was dropping. Who knows, it might be down perceptibly by Monday or Tuesday, and she'd ask Darroch Fordyce if he could get some local woman to fill in for a few days till Cosh could get back, and she'd blurt it out and take off. She slipped out quietly, not to disturb the children, and made her way up the Lookout stairs.

The room was flooded with light from three of its four windows. She thought, not for the first time, she'd like to be an artist to capture this on canvas.

From here, beyond the river, the countryside fell away from Craigievar and the Alps, and the sun was rising over the rolling downland. The Pacific would rim that land, a hundred miles away, but there the same tides that washed the shore at Timaru would be washing against the painted hull of a small yacht on a leisurely cruise among the islands that studded that tropical sea. On that was Lennox, all unaware, Lennox the reason why Rebecca Menteith, the physical duplicate of his one-time fiancée, could spin no dreams about remaining here in these fearsome, enchanting solitudes.

The sun was a blinding orb and against it the outlines of dark foothills were just a silhouetted line, but the rays struck the snow-cloaked peaks all around the west, and turned them to opalescent colours. It was as if for the brief magic of the dawn hour, the mountains were alive, striking back a myriad facets of light, living jewels with the essence of countless sunrises imprisoned within their snow crystals.

Without knowing, two words broke from Rebecca's lips. 'If only ... if only....' she almost groaned.

She couldn't believe it when echo answered her. 'If only what?' it said behind her. She swung round. Darroch was looming in the narrow doorway of the turret. 'If only what?' he repeated.

She said coldly, 'I never sell my thoughts. Not even for the proverbial penny. Not for a mint full of money. I came to see if the river had fallen.'

His voice sounded strange. 'Do you want it to fall, Becky?'

Hers was sharp. 'Of course I want it to fall. My days here are numbered, so the sooner the better.'

'Because of what I brought up last night? Do you now want to leave the field clear for Meg? Did I make you feel a heel? Because I've come to the conclusion my young cousin won't thank me at all for interfering. I didn't mean to; I seemed to get involved against my better judgement. I'll have to ask you not to leave because of what I said last night. Not till Lennox comes back and hears what you've done ... and been ... here. So you *must* stay till then.'

Her voice was steady but flat. 'I can't accept that from you. It doesn't concern you. I've got reasons you don't know about for wanting to get away from here that at present I can't discuss with you. I will, I promise, before I go, Darroch. Please don't ask me anything more now.'

She wanted to run from the scrutiny of those light brown eyes. But it would mean pushing past him, and he filled the doorway.

He said, 'Tell me one thing, Becky. Is it as much because of me as because of Lennox's disappearance that you want to leave here?'

They measured glances. She couldn't know what was in his mind. She didn't dare ask. She appeared to consider it, then, 'I can't—and won't—answer that. Because

—oh, never mind. Be satisfied with the fact that I'll give you my reasons before I leave. I can't stay once that river goes down. I would like you to give some thought to who you'll get to look after the children when the river goes down and I can go ... go home. Please have someone in mind.'

'If you go ... when you go, if Len should ring from Fiji what do I tell him? I'd been hoping to tell him what you've done for us here so he can know he had something to come back to. I think even Aunt Davy would approve of you now.'

She said slowly, 'He knows where to find me. But I doubt if he'll want to. I think he'll be genuinely relieved to find me gone.' (She just had to act as if she was Becky ... just in case, though so unlikely, Becky changed her perverse mind yet once again.) 'He did say, in that guarded wire, that he was taking my decision as final. That way, it may mean he'll come back to Meg.'

There, she hadn't slammed the door quite shut. Becky and Lennox had minds of their own, and people's behaviour was often unpredictable.

Now she said, more crisply, 'What an hour to be discussing things like this! I'm all for breakfast now. I'd like a good start.' She waved a hand towards the window. 'Glorious and all as this is, isn't there something about red sky at night, shepherd's delight, red sky in the morning, shepherd's warning? Will the Four Peaks and Heronscrag folk risk it?'

He looked past her. 'It's not really red. Not angry. It's just our startling dawn colours—refraction of light off the peaks. I listened to the early forecast. It's good for today and tomorrow. I thought it would do us all good to have company other than our own. We get too introspective on our own. I've rung Four Peaks. Gwillym can spare the time and he's the pilot. They're bringing their kids' sleeping bags and they'll all stay the night and go home late tomorrow morning when we can expect the weather to be reasonably good.

'It closes in so early in the mountains at this time of year. If they come just for today it will be a very short day. This gives us the whole evening to relax in and chat, perhaps even dance. By the way, not a word to Joanna and Verona that you may not stay on. I'm a great believer in letting time resolve things. It will take only one ring from Lennox to you to put a different complexion on things, I'm sure.'

She gave a strange laugh, said, 'I've a feeling you could be right at that. Now let's at the breakfast and I'll put those casseroles in the slow oven.' She followed him down the stairs.

It was an exciting and surprisingly joyful day. Rebecca found she just loved Verona and Joanna, and their husbands were mountain men with a huge capacity for enjoying both their food and an unexpected weekend off.

Rebecca's only worry was lest she put her foot in it with some point of view expressed differently to them when Becky had visited them, or appeared to have forgotten something that ought to have been remembered vividly, but after a while she gained confidence.

The children had an uproarious time, mainly playing outside, and the grown-ups were glad of the playroom when it became too cold to stay outside. It was a huge higgledy-piggledy house, of course, added on to by each generation, and Duncan went back to the men's quarters, and all the boys were allowed to sleep together in a big bare room that was lined with bunks used for visitors when droves of them descended upon Craigievar.

Verona laughed. 'People are always pitying us for being so isolated, and for sure we can be at times like this when the rivers cut us off, but we hardly seem to get a month when someone isn't staying—stock and station agents, lamb buyers, travellers, trampers, friends, relations. I sometimes think city folk don't entertain half as much. I only hope those children settle down early tonight. I'm looking forward to a nice long yarn when the last goodnights are called. There's nothing much on TV tonight and anyway, we can look at that when we're on our own. Becky, you've done what we all do, succumbed to the spell of the mountains, good for you.'

Rebecca caught Darroch's eye, hastily disengaged hers. The men decided they'd go off to their quarters to play cards and seemed most sincere about it. Miraculously the children were tired out and settled down. Joanna said, 'Let's have a dance. That way Becky won't feel all glamour is cut off once you've crossed the Rubicon! And it'll be ideal. Three men, three girls. Not like that night at Heronscrag long ago when it was four men and little me! I almost dropped from sheer exhaustion.' She looked rueful, said, 'I've got to admit I planned just this. I rang Verona and said to put in a long skirt or dress. How about it, men?'

They were all for it and the three girls whirled away to Joanna's room to change. Verona said, 'Becky, put on that deep blue dress you wore to the Deerstalkers' Ball in Tekapo. I thought that was delectable, just the colour of your eyes.'

Rebecca was becoming aghast at the ease with which she lied these days. 'It needs cleaning. I brushed against the lock of the car door when I got out back here and I wasn't game to try to get it out myself. Oil is hard to eradicate.'

'Very wise. The cleaners hate amateurish attempts, makes their work so much harder. What else have you got? Something glam? I love dressing up. Makes us feel we have the best of both worlds.' She went along to Rebecca's room, rummaged in the wardrobe. 'Oh, this is lovely, a deep turquoise. What a soft, shimmery material.'

'Like a *paua* shell,' said Joanna. 'You must wear this. We'll knock 'em out. I've got gold, Verona's got green, it's wonderful with her chestnut hair. Would you let me loop your hair up, Becky? I was looking at your profile during dinner. I don't know why you wear it loose ... it hides that lovely line of chin.'

Becky laughed. It was suddenly all glorious fun and to the devil with doubts and fears. Here were others of her own sex to revel in clothes, perfume being sprayed on, Joanne's dexterous fingers brushing her hair upwards till her scalp tingled; time to put on more make-up than usual in this workaday world of a big sheep-station; even the gentle warmth of these centrally-heated rooms seemed to shut out the stark conditions and remote setting of that snowy mountain world without.

Joanna stepped back, surveyed her. 'I've not lost my touch. You know, of course, that I was secretary-companion to Maria Delahunt once. She had me take a course in hairdressing so that on less formal occasions, I could groom her.' Her eyes narrowed. 'Well, how strange, I thought like Verona, that your eyes were pure sapphire. But they're not. They're turquoise too. Must be that dress. They've got a decided greeny tinge. I'd never have believed it.'

Rebecca laughed in what she hoped was a natural way, not uneasy, said, 'Yes, it's wearing this colour has that effect. When I wear emerald they hardly look blue at all. Makes me feel a chameleon. Joanna, that gold is so right for you. Now I thought your eyes were plain brown, but in that they've got gold lights in them. Eyes are funny, aren't they? Passports put them down as blue, grey, brown, hazel. Yet they all vary. Like comparing my dad's eyes with Darroch's, for instance. Both are brown, but Dad's are almost black, whereas Darroch's are tussock-coloured, sort of tawny.'

Joanna nodded, but Rebecca thought she gave her a very shrewd look. No, she was just nervous, imagining things. Verona said, 'And although Lennox's eyes are blue, they're different altogether from yours. Sea-blue, his

—sailor's eyes. Odd that he settled here. I used to stay with his parents for holidays when I was in my teens, at Island Bay in Wellington. He was much younger but even then was always fussing round with boats. His mother's father was a sea-captain. However, Lennox's future seems to be in the mountains.

'I had the feeling that if you felt this was too remote, he might settle for the coast, but now you've come to love them, just as I did. I wasn't a bit like Joanna, she fell in love with the Alps at sight, then for Matt. Oh, listen, they're getting impatient. Don't they know we high-country women need to have time to prink ourselves up a bit once in a while?' She opened the door, called out, 'We're coming!'

The look on the men's faces excused the delay. Darroch joined the two husbands in the wolf-whistles. Rebecca would have been less than a woman not to have enjoyed the appreciation in his eyes. It was foolish, knowing what she knew, but she had a feeling this was her moment and hers alone, not Becky's, his cousin's fiancée.

As it was, he felt he was liking her against his will, against his former, possibly better judgement. She disengaged her eyes and caught the same look on Joanna's face she'd seen before. It was a split second of inner revelation, and she caught her breath. *Joanna thinks Darroch is falling for me in Lennox's absence and thinks it could mean trouble.*

On the heels of that came the thought that none of this would have happened had she not been such a crass idiot, not to mention smug, thinking she could save this situation as she'd saved others during Becky's turbulent and selfish life. She hated herself now. She knew she'd done Becky less than good service in shielding her so much. It had made her feel superior, a do-gooder, always ready to pick up the pieces. It hurt to realise this, but when that fateful river could be crossed, she would vanish from their ken and in the rest of her life she would try to be more humble, hold herself back from trying to save situations.

Darroch, to the strains of a haunting melody, took her in his arms, and moved slowly into the middle of the floor with her.

She gave herself up to the rapture of the moment. She didn't deserve it, but this was all she was going to have to remember of physical contact . . . the muscular leanness of a mountain man against her, his hand smothering hers, that well-cut mouth and tanned chin so close to her whenever she lifted her head, that faint attractive hint of after-shave, his voice, that deep voice saying, 'I think you'll agree, Becky, we have our more glamorous moments among the mountains, as well as when we go down-country for dances and balls and weddings. We ought to have got you round them more than we did, but it was busy and the weeks flew by. Gwill's plane is a godsend for lighter moments as well as the more fearful ones.

'Best of all they hope to get the small bridge that will link Dragonshill with Heronscrag through by next February or so—given time free of flood—that means the Greenwoods won't have to ford the Waimihi to get out and if we improve our track to Heronscrag, we'll not be nearly so isolated. It's a long way round, certainly, but the fords between there and here aren't nearly as dangerous as this one in flood. That'll make it a lot easier on the women of Craigievar in time of sickness, or in pregnancy. Lennox'd make it plain to you, I suppose, before he ever brought you here, that we play it safe in those times. Sylvie goes down to Timaru for weeks beforehand. But she still wants another child, bless her. Did he explain all this?'

She took a chance. 'Yes, of course, but in all fairness to——' she had to catch back the next words and felt weak. She'd so nearly said, 'In all fairness to Becky . . .'

She tried again. 'In fairness to women who might feel afraid, that *is* a big consideration, the fear of accident or premature birth. But you warned me of all this that first serious talk we ever had, not only Lennox. Women have to face these things, so they must think about them.'

He seemed to hold her closer. 'Naturally. At times here it's hell for the menfolk too. They can be afraid for their men who work here, some taking foolhardy risks on the bluffs, some having quite unforeseen accidents happen to them. The men can be tense with fear for their women and offspring. But we keep up with first-aid practices; that doctor friend of Gwill's is up here once a year and renews our stocks of medical supplies. He's a grand fellow and put himself through college on his earnings up here as a shearer. I know you turned queasy when Len showed you the medical kit, but to a greenhorn they seem more fearsome at first. Give it another go with me some time. Second time round is better. Any woman up here needs to know how to take over in an emergency. Stitching up a youngster isn't as bad as it seems, because you use a local. If you had that knowledge under your belt by the time Len comes back, it could help with the reconciliation. You're worrying about the finality of the sound of that telegram, aren't you?'

She could have screamed. It was to no purpose ... she wasn't Becky, she wasn't staying. By next weekend she hoped to be gone!

Fortunately Darroch said, laughing, 'What a conversation for what's supposed to be an occasion of glamour and romance in the high-country! If Joanna had any idea what we're talking about she'd skin me. She'd say it was worse than talking sheep and cattle at a dance. As it is she's got a most peculiar look on her face, I'm sure she suspects I'm murmuring sweet nothings into my cousin's fiancée's ear!'

Rebecca wasn't surprised at the peculiar look. Joanna was amazed at the way Darroch had come round to not just approval of his cousin's choice, but was acting with noticeable tenderness towards her. It was a sticky situation. However, it would soon be over. She hoped Joanna wouldn't comment on it to Verona. She wanted no talk in the district after she'd gone. Darroch had to know the full truth of it, but he'd feel such a downright fool she was sure he'd not spread abroad the fact that Becky's cousin had taken her place. No, he'd just say Becky had found, after all, she couldn't face this for the rest of her existence and had departed, and in time the whole episode would sink into oblivion. Perhaps, in time, Lennox would marry this Meg, whom he might see in a new light compared to the unstable Becky.

How delightful Matt and Joanna, Gwill and Verona were, dancing with stars in their eyes, supremely happy with their lot, enjoying every moment to the brim. How Rebecca would have loved them for neighbours and friends.

Darroch said, 'You're looking wistful. What is it? Wanting to dance again with a better dancer than I? Gwillym is the best dancer in these parts, and the best singer. Due to his Welsh blood and natural sense of rhythm, I guess, or is it just that you wish your Lennox was here? I can understand that.'

She looked mischievous. 'Oh, you make a very good substitute, cousin-to-be ... how very ungrateful of me it would be to wish you were anyone else!'

He laughed, swung her round as they nearly cannoned into one of the other couples, 'You turn a neat phrase, Cousin Becky. That record's nearly over. I'll put another on.'

'No, I think we might put supper on soon. Matt said he'd like to hear the late news and weather. We could watch while we nibble. Verona brought over some sandwiches for toasting and Joanna has sausage rolls. You're in luck. And their pavlovas are dreams ... isn't it absurd, flying such fragile confections in? Soft-centred, crisp outside, and filled with delicious fruit and cream. I've never made a perfect one yet. I've an ambition to try these if they'll give me the recipe. Before I leave here.'

His arm tightened involuntarily. 'Then you've plenty of time. I'm not letting you go till Len's back—I wouldn't dare. Now you've proved you can take this life.'

'You *must* take me seriously, Darroch. I want you to make tentative arrangements for someone to take over here. I mean it.'

'Well, the river makes you prisoner just now, so we'll talk about it when the water goes down.'

'I'm getting very proficient on Ambling Andy these days, so you'd better begin to realise I mean it. I must get away. Before you can take even a truck through, I might make my escape on him if you refuse to entertain the idea. And get you to send my stuff on.'

'You daft creature! Nobody crosses that river till I say so. You aren't exactly the equestrian Princess Anne is, you know, though you're coming along.'

The news item came right at the end of the news session. Worst of all it was a devastatingly clear picture. Sometimes here, because the pictures were bounced back from immense mountains, the edges were blurred. But this was a good night for vision.

The announcer said, 'A cruise ship, the *Islander*, was involved in a dramatic rescue only a few hours out at sea. She picked up five members of an overturned fishing-boat and brought them back to Auckland. Our Auckland reporter interviewed some of the rescued fishermen as they disembarked.'

They were all interested, naturally, but no more than that till suddenly, as the reporter asked passengers for their accounts of the rescue, their attention was absolutely riveted.

Rebecca found herself staring at a replica of herself ... *no less than her cousin Becky.*

CHAPTER SEVEN

REBECCA'S gasp of dismay was echoed by five other gasps of surprise. Rebecca dared not close her eyes, though she'd have liked to blot out the entire sight from her vision.

She held her breath. What would be said? The reporter, mercifully, didn't call her Becky. He said, 'Miss Rebecca Menteith, a much travelled passenger, says that never before has she seen a wreck and rescue.' Becky's voice came in, 'It was really very thrilling. All these magnificent seamen risked their lives to save the lives of others. It was like something on a film.'

Typical, really, thought Rebecca, because from now on she'd have those magnificent seamen waiting on her hand and foot.

Two other women added remarks, more graphically, then a Kingsley Payne. *Kingsley Payne*—that name Uncle Alan had mentioned. There couldn't be two of them.

'Kingsley Payne is an executive member of the company who charters these cruises, and is on board as a travel consultant. He also is a world traveller, was once attached to the diplomatic corps but said it was a new experience for him also and very dramatic. Here he tells it in his own words. . . .'

When he had finished, he put his hand under Becky's elbow and moved away with her. So that was why Becky had gone on that cruise! Darroch almost switched off before they could get the weather report, he was so astounded. Then, 'I thought you told the children that people who know you well don't mistake you for each other, but she's the living image of you, Becky!'

She was still so shaken with relief that the reporter had called her cousin by her full name, she could hardly speak. She managed, rather feebly, 'Oh, side by side there are differences that show up. Our voices are rather different and we do try to accentuate what we know isn't alike. Oh, dear, that sounds muddled.'

Joanna sensed something. 'I can understand how you feel, Becky. I don't think I'd like it, to have someone so like me would somehow rob me of individuality, I think. So you'd be glad to find some differences. Your voice is certainly more crisp.'

Rebecca nodded. She hadn't looked at Darroch directly since it had happened, but she did now. At least he didn't look suspicious. She didn't want to be bowled out in front of these dear people. She wanted a chance to own up, at the right moment, when the way to civilisation was clear. Darroch said, 'Not much of a statement from a newspaperwoman, was it? Forgive me, Becky, but that was a very lightweight comment. Oh, perhaps she didn't want to hog the show, but you'd have thought she could have said something more than that.'

Verona said shrewdly, 'Well, television and newspaper reporters are competitive, Darroch. She'd probably write up a pretty meaty account for her paper and wouldn't want it to sound like a repeat. She'd probably have something more graphic written up by the time they got back to Auckland and slip ashore and phone it up. That man who took her away, is she engaged to him?'

Well, Rebecca knew the answer to that. 'No, she's not engaged to anyone,' meaning herself.

Verona sounded surprised. 'Didn't you see the flash of her ring when she lifted her hand?'

Rebecca felt low. Becky must still be wearing Lennox's ring. Surely she didn't still consider herself engaged to him? She had sounded so final. Not that you could see Becky, who loved jewellery, returning a ring. Oh, be fair, Rebecca, she hasn't had the chance. Perhaps she'd wanted to meet Kingsley again wearing a ring, seeing he'd once turned her down.

She said, 'You must be more observant than I. She certainly wasn't engaged when I left home, so if she is now, it must be recent. I daresay when the river goes down and we get mail again, my mother or my aunt will have written to tell me.' Safe to say, she wouldn't be here. She hoped no one suggested she rang her people to find out. None did.

Nevertheless she had a bad moment when the phone rang right then. Heaven send it wasn't anyone from home to ask had she seen the item! But they'd be guarded, they knew she was masquerading.

Darroch said, 'Jo, you're nearest, answer it, would you?'

When she said, 'Yes, you're right, this is Joanna, we're here for the weekend. We flew in with the Richards,' Rebecca relaxed, but only for a moment because Joanna went on to say, 'Do you want Darroch, Meg? Oh, you want Lennox ...?' Joanna gulped. They saw her do it. Then she said as lightly as she could manage, 'Oh, hadn't you caught up with that bit of news? Well, it all happened quite suddenly. You know Len was interested in that yacht trip round the Pacific, but turned it down? Well, evidently they had great difficulty getting a really proficient crew together and the family here persuaded him to go, that he could be done without just now.

'It's a bad time of year and Ewan will be back soon, so off he went. We didn't know either. It was a case of get down to Timaru as fast as possible and fly to Tauranga. He wouldn't have time to call in at Pukewhetu on his way.' Joanna took a breath and looked rather pleased with herself.

The phone crackled and they all heard Meg's voice, so Joanna must have taken it away from her ear so they—mainly Darroch—could hear. It said, 'Then perhaps that's why I've just seen Becky all done up to kill on board a cruise ship. Were you watching the late news? Is she off to join him somewhere in the Pacific?'

Joanna gave a chuckle that could have passed for real amusement. 'That wasn't Becky. Didn't you know she has a cousin, a double cousin—who looks as much like her as Verona's twins look like each other? Becky's here, right this very moment. She and Rebecca ... they were both named for their grandmother ... have been mixed up for years. I think the one we saw on TV is about a week older. Amazing, isn't it?'

This time they didn't hear Meg's reply. She must have dropped her voice when she knew Becky was there. Joanna went on, 'You'd know Sylvie was in hospital, of course? Yes, Darroch would let Queenie know. She's doing fine. Must have slipped his mind with all the anxiety about Sylvie to mention Lennox being away. Becky's coped and coped well. Easier for her to be the only woman in the kitchen. That was one thing I was spared, of course. As I was the only woman on the station when I was marooned there, they had to have my cooking or do it themselves and they were out snow-raking most of the time, so at least I fed my failures to the pigs and had no other woman to look askance. Besides which, I just had to experiment. Sylvie's a pet, but most of us would rather blunder on alone.' Joanna went on chatting, asking after this one and that, made a gesture to Darroch to find out if he wanted to take over, something that was turned down most vehemently, and then, to everyone's relief, the receivers went down.

Joanna dropped into a chair, said, 'Phew, a sticky moment.' Then she said, 'Sorry, Becky, but you know how it was, I'm sure.'

Darroch said, 'Oddly enough, she hadn't realised till I told her the other day. Not to worry. These things happen time and again, and things sort themselves out. That sounds prosaic, I know, but it's no use agonising over this. It's not a broken engagement you're responsible for, Becky, just one of those attachments that faded out, evidently, when the real thing came along. You couldn't have known when you met Len. More coffee, anyone?'

The subject was dropped. They were evidently sorry for Meg, but Lennox, they felt, now loved Becky and while they'd had doubts at first, she was now coming to stand more highly in their regard. They'd no idea there'd been a rift in the lute, that Lennox had decided to cut his losses. In time, when he came back here, he would probably turn to Meg again, and if her pride didn't get in the way, it was likely they would marry.

She would just have to consider it as a season of infatuation. How she herself had complicated things! Rebecca didn't think for a moment that Becky was going to try to meet up with Lennox. She was on board for one reason and one only, and that was because Kingsley Payne was.

It was a happy idea of Matt's to put on one more dance. They'd exchanged partners all night, of course, but by mutual and unspoken consent they took this one as Matt and Joanna, Verona and Gwillym, Darroch and Rebecca.

It was Verona who suggested a song when it was over. 'Becky, do give us a treat like that day at Four Peaks when Lennox got you to sing. Jo and Matt weren't there.' Verona turned to them. 'She ought to have had her voice fully trained, but with her parents jigging all over the world, the chance was let slip. But she must use it up here. We haven't too much local talent. Please, Becky!'

Rebecca had a pleasing contralto voice, no more. Becky's was superb. She had been too lazy to bring it to concert standard. Her parents had offered to put her under the same teacher who had trained Kiri Te Kanawa. Now Rebecca was going to be bulldozed into singing. They'd think her so churlish to refuse. They'd have to think this was an off day for her, that she was out of practice, rusty.

Joanna went to the piano, turned over music. They

chose, 'I think that I shall never see a poem lovely as a tree.' It suited Rebecca's voice. She said before beginning, 'We've talked so much today, I'm very husky. In fact I hoped I wasn't starting to get a sore throat, so I hope you'll excuse me.'

It was pleasing though, and they begged for an encore. She thought, then said, 'This will be something you haven't heard. But I know it by heart, so I can play for myself. I've a feeling it would suit these surroundings. The mountains, the streams, the sense of continuity in the pioneer history. My——' she stopped short. She'd so nearly said 'my brother'. She continued, 'My cousin Jonathan, Rebecca's brother, set it to music for me. It's called *Immortality*. It was a poem I liked.' (She had written it.)

She played a bar or two, glad she was sitting with her back to Darroch. It would be for him she was singing it.

'This loveliness that stirs my bounding heart
    To songs of praise has always blossomed here;
When Earth was young, unscarred by war and hate
    These self-same streams went singing, crystal-clear.
These mountains caught and held within their folds
    Cloud-shadows, dappled grey and indigo;
Someone, held spellbound on this emerald hill
    The same delight in God's sweet world would know,
So, when this pasture knows my feet no more,
    When all my earthly gipsyings are done,
There will be other eyes to watch with awe
    The timeless magic of the setting sun.
I would bequeath to all who follow on
    My rare delight in leaf and bloom and tree,
For in their worship of the world I loved
    My soul shall find true immortality.'

At the end of her song there came a silence. She knew it as a tribute to the beauty of the words and tasted the savour of that compliment to what she had created a year or more ago, with a thankful heart. One more thing to remember.

Darroch said quietly, 'Thank you, Becky. I think that meant more than when you were in full voice last time. It wasn't just one more song to sing, but you liked the words so much you had them set to music. And it certainly does suit here, this place we love. On which note we must go to bed. We can stack the dishes in the washer and leave them to dry till morning. You other four make your way to bed. Don't spoil your magic evening with any prosaic chores like setting breakfast tables.'

They made no protests. They took it for granted Becky would help him. They were strangely silent—comfortable silence.

He walked up the warm, long hall with her and to her surprise turned into the little passage with her, that led to the children's rooms and hers. She looked up at him, saw the corner of his good-humoured mouth twitch. 'I'm seeing you home,' he said. 'No, I want you to see the moonlit view from the little window at the end of the passage. It should be something. I saw it from the porch end when I was seeing if the cats were all right. It's my favourite ... an almost full moon over Craigievar Crag. It looks like the Rock of Gibraltar, which I once saw outlined by moonlight and electric lights as we came through the Mediterranean. It gives me a secure feeling that crag. Like in the song you sang ... it will still be here when my children's children are dust and ashes. Does that sound too gruey?'

'No, Darroch. It sounds poetic to me.'

He turned out the light, drew back the green velvet drapes.

For a moment she was hushed to silence by the beauty of the starlit, moonlit night and the dark mass outlined against it, then she said, 'It's so like that picture you have of Craigievar Castle. Almost an identical silhouette.'

'Yes, my great-great-grandfather named it for that.'

He turned away with her, walked her to her door, said, 'I think we gave them quite a romantic evening, didn't we? It's so necessary up here, to take what we can get. Softens the grimness.'

She answered without thinking, spontaneously. 'It's a good idea at any time for any couple to preserve moments of romance. I don't like the word grimness being used about here. Magnificent rather. Scenery on the grand scale, spectacular, not grim.'

'*How* changed you are, Becky, how changed.'

She caught her breath in. How foolish to be lulled into forgetting! He heard the intake, misunderstood it. 'I'm a blundering fool. Len's so far from you, and estranged. And I talk of romance!' He gave a strange short laugh, said, 'Let me be his proxy. Your imagination can do the rest,' and he bent down, brushed his lips over hers, and left her.

She stood there, clinging to the jamb of the door, while all sorts of emotions and longings swept over her, most of them physical. Rebecca hadn't reached twenty-five years without a few transient attractions, but no kiss had ever stirred her like this, yet it had been so fleeting. She had rarely known envy, but right at that moment she knew the fiercest envy possible of those other couples, Matt and Joanna, Gwillym and Verona. They lay beside the ones they loved, they'd had a romantic evening ending, probably, in lovemaking, a blend of love and passion, reaching the heights, between two people who knew all the arts of it, and knew each other well enough so that each response would be tender and satisfying.

Whereas all she got was a kiss from the man she loved as a substitute for one from his cousin. And all that lay ahead of her? A showdown ... and that quite soon.

Sunday was a glorious day. No knife-edged wind blew from the peaks, not a cloud marred the sky or veiled the tops. The sun had a caressing warmth to it.

Verona's eyes took in the sweep of the horizon; she said, 'If this continues we'll get a big thaw. I wonder if it could be possible the snow is over. But better to come now than in November when we lamb up here.' She stretched, yawned, said, 'In no time we'll be able to garden again. Even now this ground doesn't seem so iron-hard to me.' She pushed aside a scrubby alpine plant by a boulder with her foot, 'Oh, look, Becky. That crack in the ground, see! A tiny triangle of green is peeping through, the first daffodil spear is showing. Your garden is a little earlier than ours. What a life-force it must be to thrust up through soil that's half ice. Though some plants even split rocks. Isn't that tiny saxifrage called the rock-breaker?'

Rebecca, enchanted, said, 'I'm going to jot that down. It could symbolise life up here. The taming of the wilderness by little growing things. If I don't jot I so easily forget.'

Darroch's voice behind her asked, 'You mean for what you're writing about Craigievar?'

She whipped round. 'Creeping up on us like that! We could have been saying anything.'

'Oh, if it had been girls-only talk I'd have crept tactfully away.'

Verona laughed. 'You nit! As if anything embarrasses you mountain men. But what's this about Craigievar?'

Darroch answered for her. 'A bit of her cousin's journalistic skill must have rubbed off on Becky. She's putting one or two articles together on certain aspects of life up here, combining it quite skilfully with the early history. Her cousin's paper runs feature series like that, but Becky doesn't like submitting to her cousin. I can understand it, especially when their names are so similar— well, the very same except she gets the short version. I daresay too, seeing the cousin is so well established in newspaper work, that she's got an inferiority complex about attempting writing. I'd say go ahead and try the Christchurch *Press* or *Star*. This cousin sounds a very self-sufficient creature . . .'

Rebecca felt startled. She hadn't said much about her supposed cousin, but Becky must have.

Verona took it well, said, 'How awful to have a super-efficient cousin who looks exactly like you. It needed being left on your own up here to give you the chance to show what you can do. Darroch's so much more a bracing character that you'd just have to show him, wouldn't you?'

Darroch chuckled. 'I just love being talked over as if I wasn't here! Though if I hadn't been you'd have said abrasive, not bracing.'

'I might at that.'

Joanna was chuckling too. 'You're one of us now, Becky. We can say what we like to you. Do forgive us for being so beastly polite to you when you first came up here. We all know you've got to be the right type to live up here, otherwise it'd be hell for both man and wife. Frankly, we were terrified it was just infatuation with Len, especially when you were such a looker, but we don't think that way now.'

'On which note,' said Matt, who'd appeared behind Darroch, 'we'll go and do other things. People are getting so devastatingly candid we could have a real bust-up any moment. Becky's a brick to take all this, but don't chance your luck too far, my love. The kids want to have a little Sunday-school. They miss out so much in the winter.' Rebecca knew they thought nothing of going the twenty-odd miles to Tekapo to the exquisite little lake-boulder Church-of-the-Good-Shepherd on its stark hillside above the lake, with its altar window that looked out across the milky-turquoise waters and mountains of Tekapo.

Rebecca was glad she had to play for the singing, because no one could see she was moved to tears. She blinked them back. One more picture stamped indelibly on the gallery of the inward eye. Gwillym's voice with its upward Welsh lilt reading a psalm, Darroch's short but beautifully sincere prayer uttered in a perfectly normal tone without self-consciousness, revealing that this was quite customary here in the long loneliness of the winter, or summer flood-times; the unexpectedness of Nan being allowed to have her favourite hymn and it turning out to be the *Old Hundredth*, 'All people that on earth do dwell ...'

All too soon it was time for a hasty lunch-snack and the final goodbyes were said. Only Rebecca knew for certain that it really was goodbye as far as she was concerned. To Rebecca, still a greenhorn, it seemed incredible they thought a change in the weather was coming, when that sky was still cloudless, the peaks crystalline-clear against it. They said there was a feel, and a smell. Not that it would come quickly, but they must be home before any hazards could develop.

She was surprised at the sense of desolation she had as the tiny dark speck vanished from their sight. Darroch caught sight of the look on her face. 'Cheer up, lass, they'll come again. Come often enough to keep you from feeling we have no neighbours.'

Yes, they would come, but never again for her. And while she would remember them as kindred spirits, they would remember her as the girl who couldn't, after all, take the high-country.

The storm blew up as they had their evening meal, though long before that it had been snowing on the tops. Rebecca knew a new fear. If it became a blanketing snowstorm such as they so often experienced here, with deep drifts blotting out fences and rocks, they would expect from her the expertise of Becky on skis and she would have to make the abominable pretence of spraining her ankle. One more deception. But she was spared that. The snow stayed on the tops, and torrents of rain fell round the homestead area. The whole landscape became blotted out with a curtain of driving water. By nightfall the drumming of the downpour on the steep corrugated iron roof was deafening and Rebecca had a great sense of foreboding as she watched Darroch checking the long row of kerosene lamps in the storeroom, trimming candles so they would light easily, and switching all the electric blankets on early so the beds would be warm and retain their heat for a certain time if their power failed.

'But it wouldn't last long, would it?'

'It can. Rain like this wreaks havoc with transformers and so on, though breaks through rain are usually easier traced and repaired than through snow, which brings down power lines and can't be reached for days, sometimes weeks. We manage. Our worst trouble is the deep freeze. Terrible wastage of food and time.'

'How long before the river subsides after this? It was only just dropping.'

'Depends how long it keeps up. That's my least worry. This makes a terrific lot of stock-work. I must ring the hospital to find out the latest about Sylvie, in case the phone should go too.'

Rebecca hardly knew what to hope for. This gave her longer here—traitor thought—but she really did feel now with Macbeth that ' 'twere well it were done quickly'—and at least if that phone were dead, Lennox couldn't ring. She'd rather be far from here when he did. Her luck held. They had lights, power, heating, and all the conveniences so needed in a household this size, of tumbler dryer, washing-machine, iron, deep-freeze, but they lost the phone. On the news they heard there'd been a landslip in the Pass bringing down poles.

They lived in a little world of their own, not able to contact anyone. Outside the Rubicon remained an implacable barrier. If it dropped a few inches through the day, rain at night brought it up again by morning. It was a mercy the playroom was so well equipped for entertaining children who were housebound, because during many such hours, they had to be busy with indoor games and hobbies. Whenever there was a lull they got them outside for exercise and sunshine. Rebecca just had to spend more time with them, time she'd have liked to use filling up Sylvie's cookie freezer. She'd used far too much, she was sure. She took to baking at night when the endless demands from the children had ceased.

There came a night when she felt she really had caught up a little. She was going to use it to get on with the project dearest to her heart. The men settled in the lounge playing cards. She excused herself and slipped out. Up to the Lookout she went, turned on the central heating up there. It was hardly ever used in that retreat. She pulled an old table under the centre light, went to one of the old tin trunks full of papers and accounts from the old days. She must, during the days that were left to her, and they could be few once the river fell, jot down all she could from these. Some day, when the years had taken away the sting of these bitter-sweet memories, she might form from these facts a golden story of fiction about a high-country estate like this.

The book she'd planned to write in her caravan in Central Otago had lost its savour for her. She'd have to try to recapture it, because this other wouldn't be written for years. Now was her only chance to garner these historical stories, written in sweat and heartbreak, joy and achievement, by Darroch's forebears. There were diaries here written by the men and women who'd hewed out this productive holding, coped with endless disasters, sheer hard slog, faced all the irritating trials of drunken cooks who upset the men when they came in from the musters, or paused in their shearing; the accidents that had meant loss of life, or hours and days of anxiety, the early hours up loading the pack-horses to be taken to some of the distant huts, building those huts in the first place, the gigantic task of fencing; the disastrous epic stories of phenomenal snowfalls, the trials and errors of overstocking, encouraged by good summers and set back by bad winters and springs. Worst of all the toll the river took in horses when the drays got swept away, the loss of men's lives, mainly hands who were too foolhardy and crossed when crossing was perilous. The lighthearted adventures, with finery spoiled by water, and precious merchandise floating downstream, the characters that came to every station in the Depression, no-hopers and academics among them.

Darroch found her there, coming up quietly and finding her so absorbed she lifted a face to him rapt with its attention to other decades, other lives. 'Good grief, Becky! I thought you were doing more baking and went to tell you to turn it in. You're working far too hard. What does it matter if the cookie store is down? Sylvie and Cosh did it for emergencies and if this isn't an emergency, I don't know what is. But now ... are you really so keen on these articles, you're writing more?'

She laughed. 'Yes. These trunks you told me to look in are real treasure-trove. I'm supposed to be jotting, but I keep getting lost in the diaries. They lived such rich, real lives.'

He sat down with her, delved into the pile. 'I've often thought I'd like to turn this into a study, as apart from the office, such as my grandfather had in his day. Some of these diaries are his. He died when I was fifteen, and lived down-country then. But his tales were magnificent. Aunt Davy's husband was up here then. It's just become a junk-room. I think I'll make up my mind to clear it out and restore it. Would you help me with it?'

She said, 'I doubt if I'll be here.'

A heavy silence sat upon them both. Then they returned to the diaries, the photographs. The hours went by. Darroch was elaborating on the terse entries, made on days of drama and trial, when there'd been little time for writing, but he knew the stories behind the sentences.

They got sidetracked, because the politics of the day crept in. Rebecca was well versed in that, and every now and then caught herself being too knowledgeable and refrained from commenting. Her newspaper training would keep coming to the top. But why should Darroch ever entertain so wild a surmise as a change of personalities?

Vaguely they heard the two younger men depart, Duncan go off to his room. Suddenly Darroch looked at his watch. 'Long past midnight—I must let you get to bed. These past hours have just flown, we've had so much to talk about. I'd never dreamed a girl could be such a stimulating mental companion.' Rebecca didn't look up, she couldn't. But that compliment pleased her more than any she'd ever had.

Darroch said, 'It reminds me of:

"... how often you and I
Had tired the sun with talking and sent him
                         down the sky...."'

Rebecca, moved said, 'Oh, who said that? Do you know?'

'Yes. It was said more than two thousand years ago, Becky, about two and a half centuries before Christ. By old Callimachus, on hearing of the death of his old friend Heracleitus. Strange how some things last.'

She nodded, playing with her pencil. 'They live on, because they're experienced over and over in other lives, I suppose.'

Darroch Fordyce got up, pushed his chair back; it scraped roughly on the bare floor.

'Go to bed now, Rebecca,' he said. 'Just leave me here.'

CHAPTER EIGHT

THERE came a day that was perfect, with the sun striking warmly down, soft zephyrs stirring, the sound of birds returning to the high-country, and the roar of the torrents reduced to musical gurglings and rills as water still drained off rocky hillsides.

The phone was on again, they'd had the joy of hearing Sylvie's voice. She was out of hospital and staying with the Winmores. She had managed to contact Ewan in the Argentine, and now her operation was safely behind her it hadn't hurt to let him know. He would be home in ten days' time and would come straight to Timaru and stay with her till she got her all-clear, and could travel back with him, as long as Darroch didn't need him home. Anyway, if he did, he could ring them in Timaru.

The men were going up to No. One Hut with the four-wheel-drive truck and taking the children to give them a change. Their lessons, during the wet spell, were well ahead. Darroch and Lindsay were riding so they could do some reconnoitring away from the track. Darroch was disgruntled because Rebecca wouldn't come with them. 'It will make it more of a picnic if you come. Sylvie often does.'

'Sorry. It's a golden opportunity to get something done without interruption. I want to vacuum right through.'

He finally agreed, but reluctantly. 'Most mothers get a break during school hours. You've been a brick. But the men all agree it's more fun with you round.'

'Nice compliment, but I'll settle for a day on my own most happily. It will be heaven.'

'I'd never have picked you for a loner when you first arrived,' commented Darroch. 'Women have to be content with their own company once in a while up here.

141

Aunt Davina was the best I ever knew for that, always something to do when we were all up at the huts. She has a great zest for life. There are always so many things she wants to do, to study, to find out about. She'll need half a dozen lifetimes if she means to do all she wants to. She's coming back after this world trip we all insisted she should take, to help set up a retirement home for the old somewhere in the high-country. Not as remote as this, of course, but in a country township, so that men and women who have lived all their lives among the mountains won't have to go from sight of them in their old age.'

'What a marvellous thought.' Rebecca had a pang as she realised she would never meet his Aunt Davina. She packed them huge lunches. She revelled in having the house to herself, and whisked round with gusto, tidying and cleaning and polishing. A day free of school lessons was a gift from the gods. It was sheer bliss not to have to even set a table for lunch and to have only one cup and saucer, one plate to wash up. She enjoyed the luxury of reading a magazine as she ate her beef sandwiches.

By one-thirty she thought she'd earned a break and decided on a walk up Craigievar Crag, but as she passed the horse paddock Sylvie's mount, Grey Streak, came up to the fence looking for a titbit. Rebecca went to the storeroom, got apples and carrots, and as she passed the harness room saw through the open door the saddles hanging up. That's what she would do, have a darned good gallop without having to pretend she was nothing more than a promising novice at the game. They were all safely up the gully.

Grey Streak was all for it, just as Rebecca was. She had on slacks and a big oatmeal fisherman-knit sweater, so she oughtn't to be cold. It zipped up the front and had a huge ribbed collar. The mountain air would stream past her if she had the sort of gallop she was longing for. It had been maddening to have to wear Becky's mantle, dreading snow because on skis her cousin was an expert, having to pretend to be nervous of horses when she'd even done some show-jumping! Well, to hell with all that.

She was up in the saddle and off. Below the homestead was a stretch of turf free of tussock where later, they'd told her, the children would practise jumps. It continued on, almost level, open and inviting, right round the shoulder of the hill. She dug her heels in. She needn't have, Grey Streak needed no urging.

She felt the mare gather speed under her, surge ahead. The sweet mountain air took the coppery tresses from her brow, she filled her lungs with it, exulting in the glorious freedom, the untrammeled movement. This was life as it was meant to be lived, for Rebecca Menteith.

She rounded the first shoulder of the Long Gully, increased pace, her hair streaming horizontally now, making for the next shoulder. What a pace! Superb not to have to hold her in. Around the bend came a rider, coming at a fair clip, but who reined in from sheer astonishment. Not just any rider. Darroch!

As she recognised him, she got such a shock she reined in too suddenly, took Grey Streak by surprise, the mare stumbled, recovered balance, reared, came down in a depression and Rebecca sailed clean over her head and landed fairly and squarely face down, arms flung helplessly out, on a glacial boulder embedded in the turf.

Darroch was beside her in split seconds, had flung off his mount, and was swearing away. He turned her over, saw her blanched face, the blueness round her mouth, the lack of breathing, and in a moment was expertly massaging her heart. She made a movement, gurgled, struggled for breath. He turned her on her side and began rubbing her back. She gulped, drew in air, choked, then burped loudly, managed to whisper, 'Just winded. I hit here,' her hand came to her diaphragm.

He pulled her into a half-sitting position, there on the ground, continuing to rub her back. The burping continued. It was most humiliating, though at first she didn't care, it was such a relief to draw full breaths into her lungs.

Presently it was evident she was recovering and the rubbing went on more slowly. She leaned back against him and it ceased altogether. His chin was on her shoulder. He said gently, 'Are you all right now?'

She was still a little gaspy. 'I think so. Yes, I am. I—I'm sorry, you startled me. I didn't expect to see any of you till tea-time. So I pulled her too quickly. It—wasn't her fault.'

'I know it wasn't. I should just think you *would* be sorry! I died about a thousand deaths as you hurtled through the air. You just missed that jagged stump. You could have fractured your skull, broken your neck. As it is, you could have ruptured your spleen or broken a couple of ribs. What in the world possessed you to ride Grey Streak? She's not called that for nothing. And to let her get away with you?'

She opened her lips to say she hadn't let her get away, she'd egged her on, but remembered and closed them again. 'I thought I'd try her out, that's all. I could have got her under control, but I got a shock to see you.'

'You couldn't have controlled her, goose. It would take an experienced horsewoman to do that. You aren't ever to ride alone, even on Andy, do you hear me?'

'Yes, Darroch,' she said weakly.

He said, 'Before you get up, I must see if your ribs are all right. Too dangerous otherwise. Don't worry if they aren't, I've a lot of experience in ribs. I've strapped both Ewan's and Keith's. Seems to be a hazard here. But it means I'll have to look. Think nothing of it.'

She looked down on her loosened clothing. 'I'd be stupid if I made a fuss, wouldn't I, seeing you've already done a spot of heart massage?' she twinkled.

His eyes approved her lighthearted acceptance of the necessity. 'At the time you weren't capable of protesting. Turn over on your back.' He grinned. 'Hope Lindsay doesn't decide to ride in early too. If he cops an eyeful of this, heaven knows what he'll think!'

He whistled as he saw the reddened skin from the impact. 'Took it fair and square on the old diaphragm, didn't you? Sideways, a fall like that would have bust your ribs.' His hands were surprisingly gentle, even though very thorough. There wasn't even a suggestion of a cracked bone, but the bruised area, beginning to darken now, was very tender.

He buttoned her blouse as she lay, fumbling as men do with tiny buttons, zipped up her sweater. He was still kneeling. He went to smile reassuringly at her, then half way through that smile something happened to it. It just ceased to be. He looked anguished. He caught her to him, pressed her to his chest, brought up a hand to tilt her chin, then set his mouth on hers before she could begin to murmur a protest.

She was in no state to move even had she wanted to. This was all she'd ever dreamed it would be as he kissed her over and over again ... surrender, comfort, security, passion. Demanding and finding response. A giving and a receiving. This was total commitment in a kiss. It ought to have been a promise of further fulfilment to come, but that couldn't be.

The irrational moment passed. Something had to be said, excused. Darroch sat up. They remained there though, breathing heavily, not looking at each other. Then both stirred, both looked. She'd never forget the look in his eyes. The brown had darkened, the brows were down. He said, husky-voiced, 'What's happening to us? In God's name, what's happening to us? To both of us? My cousin's fiancée—I must be mad! Becky, I'm sorry. Forgive me.'

Somehow she scrambled up, clutching his arm for aid.

She said through rather stiff lips, 'Don't be sorry, Darroch. That was quite a—quite a moment. Not to be apologised for, just forgotten. It won't happen again. You aren't to whip yourself. I'm as much to blame as you. We've been cooped up together too much. It doesn't mean a thing. You thought I was going to be killed, so that was sheer reaction. Let's go. Thank goodness Grey Streak didn't run away. I hope she's not hurt.' She went across to her, ran a hand expertly over the mare's forelegs and was satisfied.

Darroch's voice behind her said, 'You've quite lost your fear of horses, haven't you? But I can't let you ride her back. We'll walk, I couldn't stand it.'

She said, 'I ought to get up again. Isn't it the done thing? And I won't gallop this time.'

'You're right, of course. But let me help you up and stay near me. Not that she's likely to rear again. I startled her.'

They walked their horses back gently to the house. They were both striving for normality. He complimented her on the spick and span appearance of the house, said, 'But you must lie down before starting the dinner.'

'I'm not going to. I'll get stiff if I don't keep moving. Darroch, don't tell the children. I think accidents could scare them. After all, their mother is in Timaru, and their father in South America. I don't want them to think I could be ill or injured either. Nan's very quick on the uptake and not half as assured as she sounds.'

'I'll leave it to you as long as you tell me if you suddenly feel you need to lie down.'

'Darroch, why did you come back early?' she asked. 'Have you something to do? If so, go and do it. I can manage the dinner.'

He hesitated. 'It was nothing in particular. Just that I ... wanted to come back.'

She knew then. He was fighting a definite attraction, one he couldn't understand himself, for the girl he thought was engaged to his young cousin. He knew that even though there had been an estrangement, if Lennox and his fiancée did part, he himself could never ask her to marry him and live here together. But she wasn't that girl, only the living image of her, and that meant the situation was equally impossible. What a curse this likeness was!

'If this weather holds, how long before the river goes down, Darroch?'

'Very soon. We're close to the source, so it floods quickly and subsides just as quickly, once the rain stops.'

A silence fell. Darroch said stiffly, 'Why? You mean ... ?'

'I mean that as soon as it does, I must be on my way. I made that break, and I must stand by it, that's all.'

He said, 'I made it worse this afternoon, didn't I?'

She turned away and her voice was muffled. 'Not worse, just harder. Darroch, please, I don't want to discuss it. Please just leave me to get on with the dinner. And I'd rather we weren't alone together again.'

He went away.

Two days later there were definite signs that the garden was coming to life. Now Rebecca could believe all they told her about it: that summer wakened the life-force in every tiny plant, every shrub, every tall tree. Duncan was a poetic man. 'The roses bloom here with never a sign of rust or black spot because we have no pollution. It's a garden as it was meant to be. It's a brief blooming compared with down-country, but perfect.'

That summed her stay here, she thought. Brief, but perfect. In setting, if not in incident. She was making her preparations now, for leaving when she could.

She resolutely accepted the fact that the hour when she made her confession would be most traumatic. For Darroch too. She sternly forbade herself to hope against hope he might want her to stay, seeing she wasn't Becky.

She knew all the reasons why he wouldn't. She would make things as right as possible. Darroch she'd have to face alone. She'd ask Duncan to take the children away, say she had something to discuss with Darroch. She must get it out without interruption. She'd ask could she even take the receiver off the hook. That was most important.

The river was dropping, dropping, but she must wait till it was as low as when she came over, and limpidly clear. Because she had to get that rental car over, not just ask them to take her in the four-wheel-drive. She'd return it to Timaru, pay her large penalty for keeping it so long. On the way, she'd stop at Pukewhetu where the Kings lived. The Hill-of-the-Stars—what a beautiful name! She must try to put things right for Meg.

What was more, Meg must know the whole truth of it, know it wasn't Becky who returned, but her cousin. That the girl on the television news was Becky, that she seemed to have finished with Lennox. That Rebecca was sure it had been nothing but a passing infatuation. She and Lennox might make it up some time.

She couldn't just drop in, though. Anyone could be there. Pukewhetu was not an isolated farm; they were quite close to Tekapo. Meg herself could be away. So she wrote it all out in a letter.

She did it in her room one night, and though she was an experienced journalist, and words were her medium, it took her hours, tearing up draft after draft. At three-thirty she actually finished it. Not that she was pleased with it, but it would have to do. She'd tried to strike a balance between revealing that she was aware Meg loved Lennox, and not telling her enough to make her realise there was a large rift between Becky and him. She had to know that Becky hadn't turned up trumps in an emergency, but that her place had been taken by her identical cousin. Who was now very sorry for her part in it. She heaved a huge sigh and sealed the envelope down.

As she did so, she heard a tap on her door. Darroch stood there. 'Becky, are you ill? Have you some delayed soreness from your tumble? I saw your light on two hours ago, it shines across the rockery outside my window, thought little of it, but woke again and saw it still there.'

His eyes went past her, saw the writing-table, the overflowing wastepaper basket. 'Hullo, it's not illness. You've been writing to Lennox! Trying to explain something.' He took a step nearer, grabbed for her hands. His eyes roved over her face, drawn in the dim light of the reading-lamp. She had on a teal dressing-gown, velvety, with a plain white nightgown beneath it. Her hair hung about her face in disarray because she'd thrust her fingers through it so often in her perplexity over the construction of her letter.

She said, 'It's not to Lennox. How could it be? We can't get mail out and we don't know where he is in any case.'

'That's true. I'd forgotten and just leapt to that conclusion. Because we can't even be sure they'll turn up in Fiji. Then who is it to?'

She said tonelessly, 'I can't tell you, Darroch. But you'll know before long. When the river goes down.'

His hands slipped from hers to her elbows. He shook her. 'You mean it's to me, don't you? Then let me read it now, girl, not just when you're going.'

She gave a mirthless laugh. 'Oh, it isn't to you. It's for someone else, but I'll tell you the gist of it when I'm going. Please, please, Darroch, don't try to make me tell you now. I wouldn't anyway, but I couldn't stand you probing. I've got to be able to pick my own time to tell you. Go to bed, Darroch.'

He fell silent, his hands still gripping her arms till they hurt. His breathing was heavy, he was so near, so dear.

He said, 'It's a hell of a situation, isn't it? Appalling, in fact. I never thought such a thing could happen to me.

I can't see any happy outcome of this. Say something, Becky, say something!'

She steadied herself by putting her hands against his chest. 'What *can* I say?' she whispered.

A long, painful pause, then he said, 'Nothing. You can't say anything. I *have* to let you go. Why couldn't *I* have met you first? Why?'

She said, 'There's no answer to that. A quirk of fate. And now, goodnight.'

Slowly he released her arms, turned without a word and went back to his room. His lonely room.

They managed, somehow, to appear quite normal next morning. Odd how steadying routine was ... breakfast and the men off to feed out, children into the schoolroom, casseroles popped into the oven, the radio lesson, the set exercises.

'Why are we doing extra lessons the last few days?' demanded Robert. 'We've plenty of time before the next set goes away, and in any case we can't get a mailbag out till the river's down.'

Rebecca said lightly, 'I thought I might be able to give you a day or two off if we got them finished ahead of time. We could have a picnic in the middle of the day for one thing, and for another, take a couple of days over at your place and get it all cleaned up ready for your mum and dad coming back. Not long now.'

They were all for that idea. They'd gone over several times to air the lovely house, and to bring things of the children's over here, but Darroch had decreed that no cleaning was to be done as once the warmer weather came and the nor'westers swirled the silt up the river beds, it would all have to be done again.

They were delighted with this idea. 'Though I like this schoolroom best,' said Nan, 'because it's bigger. That's 'cos our house is newer and costs went up. Becky, will you still teach us some days when Mum and Dad are back? It makes a change.'

All these things stabbed at her. 'I'll see.' She was going out of their lives soon and though it was nice to be missed, it was going to leave a gap for these children. But they'd soon forget. She looked at Andrew, sitting at a little desk, busy scribbling a pencil over a 'magic picture' book and beaming as a giraffe appeared. Andrew who was so like his uncle, all browns and tawny tussock colours. She'd have liked a son like that.

She heard Darroch come in and presently the phone rang. Good thing he was there to answer it. She didn't want it to be Meg, wanting to talk to her for some reason. She'd rather not have anything to do with Meg till the time came when she could leave her that letter.

Robert said he was off to get a project book he'd left in the kitchen. 'No, Robert, I'll get it. You're not rifling the cookie tin till playtime. You get on and finish that essay first.'

She moved quietly looking for it, among the racks of papers and magazines. She heard Darroch say, 'No, we've managed without all these years, we can continue to do so. I'm quite sure you can't do both, Aunt Davy. We'd only need that much if things were panning out the way we thought three months ago. You mustn't on any account tie all your money up in your nephews' interests. Who knows what's ahead? I think this scheme sounds fine. I'd be vastly relieved. It's the sort of thing you could pull your money out of if he didn't settle. But I'm sure this is right up his alley.' He turned, saw Becky, said, 'Just a moment,' put his hand over the mouthpiece and said sharply, 'This is an overseas call, would you mind letting me take it in private?'

'Of course not. Sorry,' and she fled, knew he waited till she was out of earshot before resuming. It worried her. Overseas? Aunt Davy was the one who would have put up the money for extra land for Lennox, and for building his house. It sounded as if Darroch had told her they had split up. Surely to goodness Darroch hadn't been asking her to put money into a coastal farm for Lennox, thinking Becky might then marry him? Perhaps Aunt Davina had rung from Australia.

As the day wore on and he volunteered no information at all about it, Rebecca knew she couldn't ask him. He was withdrawn to the point of taciturnity and spent the evening in his office. Rebecca had a heart like lead.

She was sure Duncan noticed it and was sorry for them both. He saw a good deal more than she wanted him to, but he was a man who knew fine when to speak, when to hold his tongue.

He began telling the children stories of his boyhood in Aberdeenshire. They listened, enrapt ... stories of guddling trout in the burns, harvesting the old way, with sheaves, and ricks being built. Stories of the Highland Games at Braemar. 'Becky here saw those, with Charles and Anne and the Queen Mother there, as well as the Duke and the Queen and the younger Princes. But in my day it was King George the Fifth and Queen Mary. Aye, they were grand days.'

Rebecca hoped he'd not ask for comment on Becky's time there. Duncan passed on to schooldays, and fishing trips, and boating on the lochs. Rebecca began to relax. Duncan turned to her. 'I noticed you dipping into that book of Sylvie's the other day, the one by Edith Holden. Are you enjoying it, lass?'

Her eyes sparkled, 'Oh, the *Country Diary of an Edwardian Lady*? that facsimile done just as she wrote and sketched it? I'm just loving it, Duncan. It has all the charm of seventy and more years ago. Those days had something, days when most girls were taught to observe things about them, and to sketch and classify. I'm so glad Sylvie is getting her children to press grasses and wild flowers, and write little bits about them. That book, of course, is exquisite. I loved the way she included her favourite poems against her sketches of the flowers and birds of that particular month.'

'How far have you got with it?'

'As far as July. I'm reading it slowly.'

'Then you've a surprise to come, lass. In August she goes to the Lake District and on to Scotland. Pass it over, would you?'

His gnarled fingers turned the pages gently. 'Here it is, lass. Listen, children. It's for September the twenty-second, 1906. That's even before your grandparents were born. She says: "Walked to the Lake of Menteith and back across the hills. Unlike most of the Scotch lochs the shores are flat and marshy and surrounded by large beds of reeds which are a great resort of Water-fowl of all kinds ... rowed across to Inchamahone Priory on one of the two islands ... the ruined walls of the Priory were green with the tiny Wall Spleenwort and Harebells were waving their purple bells aloft from many of the topmost crevices. ..." '

Rebecca was starry-eyed. 'Oh, if ever I go to Scotland, I must visit there. I'd love to see those harebells.' She stopped, said, 'I mean if ever I visit there again.' She saw Duncan look at her sharply.

Nan said, 'Why don't you get Uncle Lennox to take you there on your honeymoon, Becky?'

Rebecca said, 'It's a bit too far and too expensive, love. Oh, look, Andrew's fallen asleep in my arms. Nan, I wonder if you could help me undress him and get him to bed? It would be a shame to bath him tonight. Then you two can get off to bed too. You've had your stories from Duncan. But you can read.'

Nan kissed Duncan, then helped Rebecca. When Rebecca came back into the kitchen, Duncan knocked out his pipe on the kitchen ashpan edge, said, 'I might get away to my own bed early tonight.'

Before she thought Rebecca said, 'Oh, Duncan, don't!' Then as she realised how imploring that had sounded, she coloured brightly and stood there at a loss.

'Why, lassie, what's the matter? Have you and

Darroch quarrelled?'

She shook her head. 'No, but he seemed so moody tonight. I'd rather not—rather not——'

He smiled, the grizzled face softening. 'You'd rather not be alone with him. Now I'd ha' thought that would've been the very thing to get cleared up whatever's moithering him. He's a poor, confused laddie just now. My wife and I, now, we aye found that was the very thing, to have no third party aroond.'

Rebecca's eyes gazed candidly into his this time. 'But Duncan, it's not quite the same.'

His tone was dry, 'You mean you're not man and wife?'

'I mean we're not even—I mean I'm engaged to Lennox. I——'

'You hevna been wearing your ring this long while since. And I ken fine young Lennox must have flung off in an awfu' temper when he left. And you were downcountry. What's it all add up to, lass? You've proved yourself over and over since you came back, and Himself has a different view of you now. I have myself. You're like a different body. It's a tricky situation, aye, but time straightens out an awful lot o' terrible tangles. Do nothing in haste.'

Duncan knew that she and Darroch had been thrown too much together.

She said, 'Duncan, as soon as the river falls I'm going home. I must. There's a lot I'm going to explain to Darroch before going. I'll want him to myself for a bit. I may have to call on you then to take the children out of it. I'll—I'll ask him to tell you the whole story when I'm gone. Don't think too badly of me. I'd hate that— I've grown so fond of you. I've been a foolish impetuous girl. I've done a lot of harm and the fact that I didn't mean to is no excuse. This doesn't make sense, I know, but it's only fair to Darroch to tell him first.'

Duncan nodded. 'Aye, that'd be the way of it. You

must do as you think fit. Only don't burn any bridges. Give yoursel' a bit o' time. Darroch needs time too. But be true to yourself. Dinna snarl your life up for the sake of some misguided loyalty. Enough said. But you can rely on me to take the bairns out of it whenever you want to have that talk with the boss. You're in no state to be talking with him tonight. Neither's he. Go off to bed now with this book—it's gey tranquil. You're all eyes at the moment and thinner too. I'll make the boss his last cuppa and bring you one in too, later.'

She rose, went across, dropped a kiss on his weather-beaten cheek, whispered 'Goodnight,' chokily and went to bed.

It sounded to Rebecca like the crack of doom next day when Lindsay remarked, 'I reckon the river will be safe to cross in another couple of days. Won't it be good to get some mail?'

She decided to take the children across to Kildrummy right away. She gave the men cut lunches and she and the delighted trio cooked theirs on a barbecue over there. The children revelled in their very own surroundings again, though they were at Craigievar so much in the ordinary course of events, it had never seemed strange to them.

They let the mountain breezes blow through all day, scrubbed and polished and dusted. Rebecca's conscience was clear. If suddenly she left here, Sylvie would have no backlog of work to catch up on. She'd driven the Land Rover across so they'd taken over what baking she'd managed to do for the freezer, and filled the tins with things that would keep like ginger snaps and short-bread. It all underlined for her how short her time was.

Darroch gave her a breathing-space next day by re-marking, 'It'll be at least three more days before that river's safe. The forecast isn't too good for the next little while, but the further outlook is good, so if rain holds off in the next day or two, we'll soon be able to cross the Rubicon.'

Rebecca packed her things that night, so that when she revealed to Darroch that she was an impostor, she could get away smartly. When everyone was out of the way at the woolshed, she sneaked out to the huge row of sheds for the implements, where the hired car was garaged, and filled the boot with her gear.

She'd gone over and over the way she would broach the subject. She couldn't lead up to it, she would have to be blunt, but she'd ask him to hear her through to the end before he gathered up the vials of his wrath and let them fall upon her.

The next day the river looked very low. She said so to Darroch after lunch. 'I've been down and had a good look at it. Perhaps tomorrow it will be fordable.'

Darroch said impatiently, 'Becky, we know this river, you don't. It's not safe yet. I'll tell you when it is. Do stop going on about it.'

She gathered the dishes together, stacked them in the washer, said distractedly, 'Where on earth have those children gone? I can't even hear them. They've had a whole day off this week over at Kildrummy. They think because we've passed the timetable, I can let them get away with less than punctuality, but that's just the danger with correspondence lessons, it's so easy to get slack, and I don't want their mother to think I've let them get out of hand. I'll go and——'

Darroch turned and faced her across the huge kitchen table. 'They're not coming in, Becky. You and I are going to clear things up between us. They're off with the men. There's one thing I can't do, and that's let you just take that car and get away from here. I must know where we stand. Len's in Fiji. But he hasn't rung, so he mustn't want to. But I've got to have this cleared up between the three of us. I want him back here. I want the two of you together in front of me. You must stay till then.'

Here it came ... she took a firm grip of the edge of the table. She'd much rather have told and gone, early one morning, knowing the way was open, but she couldn't, and he was going to be furious. Why, oh, why had he broached this when that river was still impassable?

But it couldn't be impassable. Not any more. Because as she tried to remember, in wild panic, what the opening words of her confession were to be, the sound of horse's hooves on the drive outside fell into that pool of silence and as she swung round to see where Darroch's gaze was riveted, a horsewoman passed the window.

Oh, no, it couldn't be! One moment she was longing to have the hour of reckoning postponed, the next she knew she couldn't bear it to be delayed. It had hung over her too long. She said faintly, 'Who is it? Who can it be?'

Darroch said harshly, 'You know full well who it is. Perhaps it's just as well. It's Meg King, of course. She's a crack rider and knows this river better than anyone bar family.'

Meg King! The girl who loved Lennox. Rebecca's mind whirled. What now? Was this just a friendly visit, or was the purpose behind it a desire to see if this fiancée of Lennox's really had turned up trumps? She'd lost no time coming to investigate ... the river was only just ... evidently ... low enough.

Through the glass they saw Meg tie her horse to the rail, come in with quick, decisive steps, rap smartly on the door and enter even as Darroch called out, 'Come in.'

Rebecca's first thought was a despairing: 'Oh, why couldn't Lennox have fallen for her, not Becky?' She was quite lovely, with brown-gold hair and brown eyes. She wore her riding-clothes well. Rebecca guessed she'd taken extra care with her appearance and had hardly a hair out of place after a long gruelling ride, so she must have stopped after fording the river to do herself up. Good for her!

She had regality in her bearing and—Rebecca feared —purpose in her eyes.

She was very much in command of the situation. She said, 'Hullo, Darroch, hullo, Becky. Glad to have caught you together. This is what I hoped for. Tell me, are we likely to be interrupted? I'd prefer not to be. I'd like to get out what I've come to say, all in one piece.'

Darroch said grimly, 'Then I've a lot in common with you right now, Meg. I'd sent the children off with the men because I wanted to do some straight talking with Becky myself, but I'll postpone it. This could be very interesting.'

Meg looked him straight in the eye, 'Then she's not, after all, the little ray of sunshine Joanna would have had me believe? I wondered. It seemed too fantastic to——'

His voice was as cold as the ice-falls on the mountains. 'She's very much a ray of sunshine, believe me. We don't want her to leave here. We're not going to let her go. That's what *my* straight talking is about.'

Meg looked puzzled. 'The sooner she leaves the better. She knows it's all washed up. How anyone could come back here after what Lennox told her in Timaru is beyond me.' She looked directly at Rebecca.

Rebecca gasped. 'Timaru? Lennox?'

Meg made a gesture of impatience. 'You know quite well, but I guess Darroch doesn't. You've pulled the wool over his eyes, evidently. Darroch, I'll tell you what happened. I've got it all here in an airmail letter from Len, from Fiji. She ran off, didn't she, leaving a note in which she said if he loved her enough, he'd take a farm nearer civilisation?

'Len was furious. He tore after her, thnking she'd gone to Auckland, because he had things he was going to tell her. He was willing to go right up there to clear things up properly. He'd been wanting to tell her for a week or more. To his amazement he ran slap bang into her in Timaru. So he marched her off to Caroline Bay where he told her he was never so glad of anything in his life as he had been for that note she left.

'The answer was no, he wasn't taking a down-country farm. When I got that far in Len's letter, I was actually sorry for you,' she swung round on Rebecca, 'because even though you'd treated Lennox so shabbily ever since you came up here, I'd be sorry for any girl who was told what Len told you. But I'm not sorry now, my word no, because you sneaked back here, determined, I suppose, that you wouldn't be the jilted one, and tried to worm your way into the family's good graces after all. He told you he was going off for a few days to get over it, didn't feel like going back home, and you hoped if you made a hit with the family in the meantime, all would be well.

'But it had no chance of being made up because—I'm telling you both this because obviously Darroch doesn't know and we *must* get our lives straightened out—because Lennox had found out some time after you came up here ... the day you sharpened your claws on me, to be precise ... that what he felt for you was sheer infatuation and he thought it better to break an engagement than have a broken marriage. He'd also realised that the one he really loved was *me*. But you couldn't take being jilted and you're so convinced you're irresistible, thought Len would only have to come back to fall for you all over again.

'But he went on to Tauranga, found he could be taken on for the *Hibiscus* trip after all, and thought it would put a welcome space of time between breaking off his engagement to you and ... and courting me! He didn't know how I'd take it if he came back and it seemed too sudden. But why, tell me why did you stay on after he sent that wire saying he was taking it as final and going off round the Pacific? Why?'

CHAPTER NINE

REBECCA knew the hour of reckoning was upon her. She must be coherent. She must try to put things right no matter how great her humiliation, how great Darroch's disillusionment with her.

So she spoke clearly. 'I didn't. At least *Becky* didn't. *I'm not Becky Menteith*. I'm Rebecca Menteith, her identical cousin.'

The effect was almost ludicrous. Darroch uttered an incredulous sound. Meg, full of fire one moment, was white and speechless the next, and limp. Darroch, coming to himself, pushed a chair under her. He made no move to give Rebecca a chair. He switched back to staring at her.

Rebecca was glad her voice didn't falter. 'It seems incredible. It is. I know nothing of Lennox meeting up with Becky—it must have happened after I left Timaru. I'd given up my newspaper job and was going to friends in Dunedin who were going to lend me their caravan in which to write a book. My aunt was distressed with what she was hearing from Becky, and begged me to stay in Timaru, get in touch with her, and if possible come up to Craigievar to see what manner of people you were. I arrived to find Becky at the hotel.

'She went to pieces—Becky always does. She thought her father would come down on her like a ton of bricks if she broke another engagement, and I think that although she flung out of here determined to make Lennox take a farm nearer civilisation, she must have had doubts by the time she reached Timaru. She begged me to come up here so I could tell her father about what she called stark and grim conditions. Also that I might convince him the people up here had treated her badly.

Oh, I knew you hadn't—I know my cousin, she's hopelessly spoiled—well, she was so distressed I said I would. I've got Becky out of many a scrape in schooldays and I'm afraid I've been smug about it. So I was due to come a cropper, and serve me right.

'When I got out of the car and Darroch took me for Becky and hoped—very sarcastically but still hoped—that I'd come back because I'd heard Sylvie had gone to hospital and I was going to put my shoulder to the wheel, I couldn't resist it. I decided to pretend I *was* Becky. Few people can tell us apart. I thought it would be only for a day or two, that I'd ring Becky in Timaru, get her up to Fairlie and switch roles back.'

Her voice, had she but known it then, revealed a little of the anguish of mind she had known when she said, 'And she'd gone. Gone without trace. I know now she'd gone to Wellington. That was Becky on that cruise, of course. That was the man she's really in love with. My uncle told me that when he answered the phone when I rang one day from here. He gave her up once. I didn't know about him. I don't pretend to understand it all. The river rose, and I was too scared ... in fact terrified to confess the way I'd taken everyone in and one thing after another happened.'

She sighed. 'It's been a nightmare. Lennox went off on a yacht and I was needed here and I loved—loved Craigievar and loved the children and they needed me, and I felt I'd involved them all. You've got to believe it was a moment of sheer madness. I thought here was a fine chance for Becky to prove herself for once. I thought she seemed genuinely heartbroken in Timaru. I think now she was only sorry for herself and scared Uncle Alan would stop her allowance and make her get a job.

'I thought if only I could retrieve the situation, I could get her back and make her see this was the chance of a lifetime to show everyone that given a challenge she could take it. I didn't know about Kingsley Payne, you see. Uncle Alan told me on the phone. I think she probably wanted to get engaged to someone when she heard he was coming back to New Zealand ... so he wouldn't find her wilting on the bough. That's how Becky's mind works. Apart from that, I found I wanted to stay, to help. A homestead and children with no woman to cook and to supervise lessons. Oh, I know it was stupid, but it was done in a flash and there was no turning back—or so it seemed.

'It's been hideous playing this part expecting to be tripped up every moment, dreading every ring of the phone, feeling false every time I was praised for my change of heart. I never dreamed it would last as long. The river wouldn't let me go, and I couldn't bear to leave the children. I told Darroch, Meg, just the other night that as soon as the river was down and he could get someone in to assist, I'd go. He thought it was because I—because as Becky—I was taking Lennox's wire to mean when he came back he wouldn't want to find me here. But I was going to tell him I was a fraud, that I was Rebecca. I couldn't face doing it till I could get over the river. He would be furious. It must be tell and go.'

Darroch, strangely white under his tan, said, 'Is that true, Rebecca? Really true? Or were you just going to leave as Becky, leaving me in ignorance? Not giving me a chance to——' He cut off. She couldn't read his expression. It was like a house with closed shutters. When his anger *was* unleashed, it would be a terrible thing.

'It *is* true, Darroch, I can prove it. You'll know now I didn't know about Meg. At the time you thought me obtuse. I can prove it because in my room I've got a letter I wrote to Meg. That was what I was writing that night. It's the hardest letter I've ever written. In it I explained everything, probably more lucidly than I've explained now. My idea was that I'd tell you, throw my last-minute things into a bag ... most of them are in the trunk of that rental car . . . and get away over the Whaka-rite without damage when the river was low enough. I was going to call in at Pukewhetu and leave that letter for Meg.

'If only I'd known Becky and Lennox had had a show-down in Timaru! It explains why she said to me, when she phoned from Wellington, that she'd been insulted and humiliated. She laughed at me when I demanded she come back, said I'd got myself into it, get myself out of it.' She turned to Meg. 'Frankly, Meg, your Lennox has had a lucky escape. Have no jealousy ever of Becky. I imagine his engagement to her has held few really happy moments. You'll think us a bright pair. I shouldn't be so scathing about Becky. You can take over here, Meg, when I go. I want you to read that letter, and show it to Darroch, because in it I said I was going to tell him who I was before I left. I'll get it now.'

She whisked away on that last word, leaving the thun-derstruck pair, who'd listened without a movement to what she had to say, seized the letter, came back with it. They'd come out of their trance and were both talking at once, but cut off as she appeared. She put the letter on the table between them. 'Read it,' she commanded.

Darroch spoke. 'Yes, we'll read it, Rebecca, but not with you standing there. I'm going to ask you to go to your room and give us a chance to read and discuss it. Now go.'

No one could have argued with a tone like that. Least of all Rebecca who had loved him and disillusioned him. She went with bent head, feet dragging. She sat down on her bed. It had gone too deep for tears. She stared hopelessly into space. Suddenly the silence with no voices bore down on her like prison walls. She'd have to go outside, draw in great breaths of the wine-like moun-tain air. Into that silence fell the sound of Meg's horse whinnying.

Rebecca lifted her head. *The crossing was safe for a*

horse. It had probably been safe for a day or two for that, but Darroch hadn't wanted her to go. He'd discovered within himself, inexplicably and unwanted, this tenderness for the girl he'd at first despised. So he'd lied about the river. Well, she wasn't the novice equestrienne he'd thought. Not a Princess Anne, he'd twitted her. Well, Becky wasn't, but Rebecca had a couple of cups she'd won at horse shows. Now was the time to take advantage of that.

She wouldn't dare risk a rental car, though possibly the four-wheel-drive truck would have taken it. But Darroch's horse was there, saddled, tethered to the fence from his ride this morning. She'd have to send for her things later. She'd just take her overnight bag and her money.

She would ride Apollo through the ford and on to Pukewhetu. She believed Queenie King was a most understanding person. She would tell her the whole story, say how delighted she was that the way was now free for Lennox to marry her niece, and would they run her into Tekapo whence she could take the bus for Timaru. They could return the horse some time. From there she would go to Dunedin, take the caravan, disappear into the wilds of Fiordland and begin that gipsy year as she had planned it for so long. It seemed aeons ago. Pre-Darroch days.

She worked quickly, sat down at the desk, wrote her brief note to Darroch. She didn't even head it properly, just:

'Darroch,
    Seeing the ford's clear for crossing by horse, I'm off on yours. I'm a show-jumper, not a novice, so it won't mean a thing to me. I'll leave it at Pukewhetu. I'm afraid I'll have to leave you to return the rental car to Fairlie—I can't risk taking it. Here's a cheque to cover the time I've had it. I'm going to Dunedin,

I'll send an address from there to have you forward
my suitcases. Meg will see you through, I'm sure, till
Sylvie comes home. You may not believe this, but I've
regretted my impulsive action almost every moment
I've been at Craigievar. Because I made a bad situation worse for you. Just wipe the Menteith girls out of
your mind. We seem to have been born to trouble, to
making trouble for those we—I mean for other people.

Rebecca

P.S. Please ask Meg to give Andrew some cough
syrup tonight. Just in case his cold goes on to his
chest.'

It was easy to leave the house unheard, unseen. There
was a side-door near her room and she could walk on the
grass till she reached the paddock, which was far enough
away.

She untied Apollo, swung into the saddle, walking him
down hill, past the woolshed, the sheepyards, till she was
out of sight of the homestead on Craigievar Crag. Then
she made more pace. She wouldn't look back. Even when
she crossed the Rubicon she wouldn't allow herself that.
She'd loved this place too well and it was all over. Better
she'd never known it, never known Darroch, then her life
ahead wouldn't seem so empty.

The sun was glorious, the day was fair. The river
wasn't as low as when she'd crossed over, because then
she'd not got even a splash inside the car, but it was low
enough because she could even see the shingle glinting
under the rippling water. No colour in the river meant
normality, she thought.

She'd often splashed through minor rivers on her
treks with the Pony Club, in the lovely bush-clad hills
around Auckland, so she let Apollo pick his way gently.
He stopped to drink at first, blowing delicately on the
surface, to clear it of leaves and insects. Then she urged
him on.

It was wider, of course, than on her first sight of it. But not too wide. They went steadily in, and the water began to gradually deepen around them. He seemed to be shying away from going straight across, bearing downstream a little. She'd heard you needed to let the horses pick their own way. Then he seemed reluctant. It was cold, of course. He needed urging on now, with heels and voice, 'Oh, come on, boy, I can't go back now, even if you don't like it. I've left a note ... that was my exit line. I don't want an anti-climax. On you go, Apollo, on!'

The current was flowing more swiftly here and he was definitely turning downstream ... that was funny, because Meg hadn't dripped any water at all, but this was over her stirrups now. It was no good him going across here, because that bank began to rise, and there were trees ... he wouldn't be able to scramble up there ... she tried to turn him round, but suddenly the horse plunged, the water came up over her knees, and the next moment Apollo was swimming strongly, turning directly downstream.

Rebecca kept her head. All her horsemanship came to her aid, though she'd never been astride a swimming horse before. She remembered Darroch saying you never looked down into the swirling waters because it made you dizzy, and you stayed with your mount. She looked at the bank near them, broken away with scoured-out willow-trees, and knew they couldn't make it there. Apollo knew he must take this deep current and make for one of the shingle banks that intersected the river further down. For one moment fear gripped her, paralysing even thought, then she rallied. Although this river ran bank to bank below the homestead, as the river valley widened out in its efforts to reach the sea, it became one of the normal braided rivers of the South Island, and there were plenty of islanded banks of shingle. She could be stranded but safe from the waters.

The water was icy-cold, snow-fed. Apollo was a magnificent horse, but the current on this side was evil and could not be resisted, they must go with it till it shelved. No use calling for help, no one knew she'd gone, no one would be within call. She kept uttering encouraging words to Apollo, relying on his instinct to get them to shallower water.

She felt the tug of the water on one side, almost drawin her out of the saddle, she had her feet ready to slip out of the stirrups as soon as she felt the horse founder ... she was drenched to the skin but what matter? ... she was lying low on his neck now, clinging.

His head was well up, but the water was breaking over them both. Her bag had gone long since—not that that mattered. Nothing mattered save survival for both Apollo and herself. Ahead she saw, on a level with her eyes, a shingle bank in the middle of the river, and Apollo was making for it. She managed to utter a few words of encouragement gaspingly, there was an awful sucking sound as his front hoofs found the shingly surface and he pulled his hindquarters up out of the river, staggered, snorted with fear, scrabbled as his hooves sank in, and with a terrific effort pulled them clear of the cruel waters. He made a gallant effort to reach the top of the bank, but began to roll. Rebecca managed to fling herself off as he went over, somehow made it, turned and grabbed at the reins as if her slight weight could possibly stop the great horse from slithering back into the water.

Perhaps the tug did give him a vestige of confidence. Anyway, he came up a few inches, and collapsed, his tortured lungs gasping for air, as he lay there.

Rebecca was spreadeagled, looking as limp as a bundle of seaweed flung against the shore by some mammoth tide. It was respite, no more, she knew. She was stranded in the middle of a river and there could be treacherous scoured-out streams as wide as many lesser rivers, between here and safety. But this was respite for what lay ahead. And she had to get herself, and Apollo, out of it.

The next instant she thought she was going mad, because she could hear voices, voices shouting, and the sound of hoofbeats. They were some distance off, she began to realise, but what a miracle, voices in the wilderness! One moment she was a sodden heap, the next she was on her feet, staring wildly in the direction of the sound.

She scrabbled madly up the shingle bank, lurching and slipping on the loose stones. She gained the top, and saw, incredibly, two riders coming towards her. Certainly there would be other streams between them, but at least someone knew she had to be rescued. But they were coming upstream, not from the homestead. They saw her figure appear on the top of the bank because they stood up in their stirrups and waved and shouted again. She must be seeing things. It wasn't Meg and Darroch. No chance of that—no time. And unless people were dropped down in here by helicopter, they just didn't appear.

She managed to wave back. More shouts. It sounded vaguely like: 'We're coming. We're coming!' Then, disconcertingly, the riders disappeared from view. She guessed, with sickening apprehension, that they'd dipped down into another stream. God send it wasn't like the torrent she'd just emerged from. She made a few tottering steps forward; she must try, she must, to see if they were all right. How terrible if she were the cause of innocent people losing their lives! Once more she'd acted with a rash impulsiveness more suited to a teenager.

It was five minutes only, but they seemed like five hours, then the riders breasted a bank and came trotting towards her, a winding way, dodging great boulders and splashing through shallow channels. Old uprooted willows obstructed their path sometimes, brought down by a hundred similar floods ... finally they reached her and flung themselves from their mounts—Joanna and Matthew.

Matthew reached her first, held out his arms, said in duet with Joanna, 'Becky! Thank God you made it!'

She clung to Matthew's arm, hardly able to support herself, said strangely, they thought, 'Not Becky, not Becky.' Then, 'I'm Rebecca. I always have been Rebecca. And I was running away from Craigievar because Darroch's found out,' then she sagged and Matthew couldn't hold her in her drenched condition, and she slithered to the stony river bed.

They knelt beside her, rubbing her hands, her cheeks, calling to her. 'Come on, Rebecca, come on!' Matt said. 'It's all right, Jo, she hasn't got water in her lungs, she's just whacked. This is reaction. I feel a bit weak myself. ... Rebecca, come on now, come on!'

She came round to the sight of two concerned faces close to hers, said, 'Apollo ... he was nearly done for. He was so gallant. Is he all right? He knew the river better than I did and I forced him in. And he's Darroch's.'

Joanna said, 'You were magnificent yourself. We saw the whole thing from the track—we decided to follow Meg. I died a thousand deaths when I saw you.'

Rebecca's lids flicked up again. 'Follow Meg? But she came over the Rubicon. That's why I tried to cross. I thought it a good way to clear out.'

'Oh, Rebecca, she was staying with us. Gwill dropped her off in the plane. The small fords between our place and yours are right down now. She said she had to see Darroch, that she'd had a letter from Len from Fiji and that this was the only way. That it wasn't anything she could discuss on the phone. I love Meg, but she had more on her mind than she told us, I thought. But we must get you warm. Oh, Matt, Apollo's getting up!'

Rebecca struggled to her feet even as Apollo did. The

great horse shook his head, then hung it down. Matt went to him, stroked him, spoke soothing words to still his trembling, then urged him up over the loose, horrible shingle, on to firmer ground and into full sun. A sob escaped Rebecca.

Joanna put an arm round her. Matt said, 'We must get Rebecca into something warm and dry immediately and to the devil with the explanations. For some reason you took Becky's place. Leave it at that. That water's icy, but there's heat in the sun. Jo, give her your vest ... she can have my shirt and jersey. Can't do anything about her trousers, though, but we'll get her home as soon as possible.'

'Yes, we can,' said Joanna fiercely, 'I'll put her wet ones on. *I* haven't been nearly drowned. I'll wear hers.'

No matter how Rebecca protested, they had their way. Nothing had ever felt as comforting as Matt's huge woollen tartan shirt and his Aran sweater. Joanna's slacks were bottle-green flannel and their roughness and warmth after the smooth chill of the water was unbelievable. Rebecca's teeth stopped chattering.

Matt said, 'You're coming up in front of me. Jo will lead Apollo. I can't risk him taking fright at these two streams we have to ford, with you on him. They're quite low, but he's been through an ordeal. And I don't want you getting another scare. Actually, he'd probably follow, but he may just balk at the sight of the water.'

Rebecca clutched him. 'We'll go to Heronscrag, won't we, not Craigievar? I can't face Darroch.'

'Impossible. I don't think you know how many miles that is. I want you into a hot bath and bed as soon as possible. Besides, Darroch will be out of his mind if he finds his horse gone and thinks you've attempted the ford. The sooner the better.'

'I don't think he'll even have discovered that yet. It may have seemed an eternity we were struggling in the river, but it's no time really. I left a note, but I think he and Meg had a lot to say to each other.'

Joanna said calmly, 'Rebecca, Darroch *will* be out of his mind if he knows you've flown Craigievar. I didn't surmise as wild a guess as you substituting for your weak-kneed cousin, but I was very worried that weekend. Darroch's had plenty of chances with the local lasses, but I've never seen him like that before. You seemed so right for each other. I was all mixed up, didn't know what to hope for. So, it'll be all right, you'll see. Look, you can explain as we go along the track when we're through the fords. Don't be frightened, they're just ripples. This is the main stream.'

She was right, they forded them with ease, though Apollo was uncertain. Then when they gained the track, cut by bulldozers into the solid side of the hill, and left largely in its natural state except for culverts, every time Joanna was able to draw abreast Rebecca told them her miserable, foolish story.

Matt would never know how much it did for her when suddenly she felt a great belly-laugh rumble up from inside him. Joanna, vastly relieved, for she was so afraid Matt might say something shrivelling to Rebecca, even a contemptuous 'Women!' joined in immediately.

Matt tried hard to subdue his mirth, said, shaking against her, 'Oh, Rebecca, how like my absurd Joanna you are! She got herself in the most awful pickle when *she* was stranded at Heronscrag. I hated the sight of her for a few days, then I fell for her against my will. So stop worrying. Jo and I will stay a day or two to get you sorted out, damned if we won't. We've got Christine and Uncle Henry staying at our place. I won't leave you and Darroch alone for a moment till I'm quite sure you've got it all cleared up.'

But Rebecca shrank against him, almost lost in the folds of his big shirt and jersey. 'You're darlings, both of you, but it won't be like that. Darroch is going to feel I made an utter fool of him. He'll think me as irrespon-

sible as Becky. I'll just try to bear staying there till the
river goes down. Oh, I've just realised my bag's gone—
my purse, my cheque-book, everything is at the bottom
of the Rubicon. Jo, will you lend me some money till
I get to Dunedin and my parents can send me some and
get a new cheque-book for me? You see, I was borrow-
ing a friend's caravan there and having a year away
from the office to write a book. Only I have to get there
first.'

Matthew said, 'Don't be a goose. Stay at Craigievar and
write your book there. The story of Craigievar. An epic
story of women who faced the wilderness for the sake
of the men they loved. It'll be worth facing Darroch's
understandable anger to begin with. He won't stay mad
with you for long. There's a place for you here. Pity
you won't be able to conclude the history of Craigievar
with the tale of how Rebecca came to the station, but
of course you couldn't for your cousin's sake. Pity, it'd
make a snazzy ending.'

Rebecca said, 'Matt darling, there's another reason
why I can't stay, one you haven't thought of. And it's
insurmountable. This is not only Darroch's home, it's
Lennox's. I'm sure their Aunt Davina will buy in the
extra land for him if he marries Meg. I'm the living
image of his first love. It wouldn't be fair to Meg, to
Lennox. It could disturb him. He would hate me. Darroch would never do that to him.'

Both Joanna and Matthew fell silent. That meant one
thing and one only. They too knew a situation like that
was beyond a happy ending for Rebecca.

CHAPTER TEN

BACK at Craigievar Darroch and Meg had finished their talk. Much had been said that would have astonished Rebecca. They both felt exhausted. There had been so much to explain, to ask, to understand.

Finally Darroch said, 'Well, that's that. You must stay, Meg. I can't allow you to go back through the river and all the way to Pukewhetu in the state you're in. Besides, it must be only just safe to cross.'

She looked astounded. 'I didn't ford the Rubicon. Gwill dropped me in at Heronscrag and I rode over from there.'

'Well, you're not riding back. I want you to stay anyway. This has, of course, been better for *you*, finding out that the real Becky wasn't here. It was gallant of you, lass, to find the courage to face Becky, and I know you did it for the sake of Lennox. You thought she was going to cling to him.'

Meg nodded. 'Yes, like a limpet, but Len really had finished with her. Only if she really had had a change of heart, it was going to be hell for everyone. We're such a close-knit community, and from being downright hostile, Joanna and Verona were almost glowing about the way she was coping. They talked on the phone to Queenie. Before Len's letter came I thought—well, that was it. She and Len would make a go of it and I'd fade out of the picture. Then the letter. It was a minor miracle to me, but the wonder and joy of it was hideously overlaid with the fear that things still might not work out harmoniously. But now it's all plain sailing, isn't it?'

Darroch's brows were down once more, his face had that carven granite look, making it hard to read, but he said slowly, 'Fair sailing for you and Lennox, yes.'

Meg looked shocked. 'Oh, how can I be so selfish? You still have problems, haven't you? Forgive me, Darroch.'

He caught her hands. 'Don't, Meg. You were so gallant for so long. You deserve all that's coming to you. Take it with both hands. Don't let anything cloud that.'

Meg reached up, kissed his cheeks. 'Thanks, Darroch. I'm getting myself a very understanding cousin. I just hope——' she broke off. 'We must get this cousin of Becky's out now. It will have seemed much longer to her. It's dreadful to feel yourself in the wrong. A day or two of a substitution like that wouldn't have mattered, but she must feel such a liar. And she knows we loathe her cousin. Darroch, should I make myself scarce? I— I don't know what to say, how to advise you.'

'Then don't try,' he said, with a smile that had no mirth in it.

She shook his arm, sensing something more troubling him. 'I know it's devilish awkward with the river up, having to have her here still, but as soon as she *can* go, she *will* go. No one would want to stay on after being found out like that.'

'That's exactly what I'm afraid of,' he said. 'But that's for Rebecca's ears only. Come with me. There's one thing she doesn't know yet, and it may make a difference.'

They went along the passage, tapped, got no answer, tapped again. Darroch raised his voice. 'It's no good, Rebecca, we've got to see you. Let us in or we'll just come in.'

The next moment he pushed the door open and found the room empty. 'Rebecca, where are you?' he shouted. He muttered something ... farm language, mustering language.

He strode out, pushing open the office door, called up to the Lookout, came back to her room in answer to a shout from Meg.

He came in at a rush, found her with a pad in her

hand, not a neatly folded note, just that scrawl on the open pad. Her tone was terrified. 'Darroch, she thought too that I came over the Rubicon. Darroch, what's it like? Tell me it's gone down even today?'

His face was as if it was carved in granite and just as grey. 'Even if it has,' he said, '*it's still too deep*.' He nearly knocked her down as he rushed for the door.

He didn't hesitate, saw Apollo was gone, already, seized Meg's mare, flung himself on her back and thundered down the hill. Meg didn't hesitate either. She caught Grey Streak with ease, was on her bare back in a trice, brought her knees in and was off in Darroch's wake. He'd reined in at the ford, had already gazed across it. There were no signs of a wet horse having come up on the far bank. You could see for a long distance along the road and it was as empty as the rest of the landscape.

As Meg came up with him he said, 'She'd never make it ... never get across. She must be downstream ... Apollo would head into the current ... she's been swept away. Oh, my God ... she may have made it to one of the strips ... it's our only hope ... come on!'

Meg shouted as she wheeled in behind him, 'She said she was a good horsewoman, Darroch, hope, hope!'

They went full pelt along the level part of the road as it ran along that bank before it would rise to the Heronscrag Track. But they wouldn't take that, they'd go along the dry part of the subsiding river, along the bed itself. They'd have to take it more slowly, because of the boulders and driftwood, but there were truck ruts in some parts where the flood waters hadn't reached. Meg was amazed nevertheless at the speed Darroch was making, despite the way his eyes were raking the riverbed from left to right. He was muttering to himself as possibility after possibility occurred to him.

He knew the terrain like the back of his hand, she knew, but when could anyone predict the changes that took over when this treacherous river had been in flood?. They came round the first bend, and Darroch didn't hear the sound of hooves on the rough road above, because he was still muttering, feverishly scanning the intersecting streams; perhaps couldn't hear it for the pounding of his heart, but Meg caught it, looked up, and yelled, 'Darroch, look above you ... horses ... and *they're leading Apollo*!'

It was a ghastly moment. They couldn't, in the first moment or two, take in that one horse carried two people, and it would have been beyond them anyway, to recognise Rebecca sunk into the folds of the enormous shirt and jersey. But there was something ... someone!

Fortunately at that point an angled track from the higher one led down to the river bed, otherwise, as Joanna said later, Darroch would have scaled that loose bank. He gave a terrific shout, indistinguishable as a word, only recognisable as extreme urgency.

The three above hadn't seen them. They reined in from sheer surprise, and waited. It was obvious nothing was going to stop those two riders charging up that cutting. They stood, the horses motionless.

Both riders reached the track, Darroch first, then stopped in front of the others. A few yards only separated them. Darroch gazed at the engulfed figure in front of Matt, said through stiff lips, 'She's all right?.' It came out as a croak.

Matt tried for lightness, said, 'very much all right, but she needs a hot bath and a change of clothing.'

Darroch slid down, took a step towards them, and crumpled where he stood, in front of his mount. Matt said urgently, 'Take the reins, Rebecca,' and was down and rushing towards his big friend. He knelt down, said, 'Snakes and lizards, *he's* flaked out on us now!'

It was momentary. Even as he said it, Darroch's lids flickered. He focused his eyes with difficulty, said, 'I have *not*. Never flaked out in my life. I—it's just relief.'

Matt couldn't help it. He laughed out loud, said, 'Best imitation of a faint I ever saw in my life. It's all right, mate, we won't tell it against you, I swear. Neither will anyone else.'

Darroch went to get up, Rebecca cried out, 'Stay where you are or you'll go out to it again,' and she slid down to the ground. That was just what Matt's horse was waiting for. He was sick of this. He took off. Joanna saw what was happening, make a grab but hadn't a hope of reaching him, and at the same moment she let go of Apollo's leading rein. Apollo decided that what was good enough for Jason was good enough for him, and followed at a good clip.

Matt swore. 'Now look what's happened! We'll all be going home tandem yet. Joanna, if you don't stay in the saddle I'll beat you!'

Rebecca knelt down in the dirt. She was indescribable. Darroch came up on one elbow. 'Look what a fool you've made of me,' he said bitterly.

She bit her lip and drew back. 'I know. It was dreadful, I ought to have told you long ago. But I hoped——'

'I don't mean *that*. I mean scaring hell out of me and making me make an ass of myself like this. Me, a high-country man!'

It was a sudden descent from the dramatic to the ridiculous. Matt saved it. He yanked Rebecca to her feet. 'Up you go in front of Joanna. And stay there! Meg, take Darroch on your own horse and I'll ride that thing you've got there bareback. I can't trust Darroch not to slip off her. Get him behind you and tell him to hang on tight.'

So Darroch swore at his friend. It had all the hallmarks of farce, Rebecca thought miserably. She was going to be bathed and changed like a toddler who's fallen in a duckpond. Then, presumably when she was lower than low, Darroch would tear more strips off her for this further folly. They plodded miserably home, even if Jo, sweet Jo, kept murmuring comforting things into her ear as they went.

Protests were of no avail. Joanna got her into a steaming bath, washed the river silt out of her hair, scrubbed her, made her lie in it and soak, when all she wanted to do was scramble out, huddle herself into some clothes, and hide herself away from the others. But Darroch was going to have his pound of flesh. He deserved to have it too.

Joanna was maddening. She took her time over choosing even the underwear. As if it mattered! 'By rights you ought to be in bed with the electric blanket on, so thank your lucky stars I'm soft enough not to insist on that.'

'Personally,' said poor Rebecca, most bitterly, 'I wish I was unconscious. It would have been heaven to have stayed out to it, to have developed fever, delirium, anything rather than have to face Darroch in the mood he's in *and have to stay here till that foul river goes down.*'

'Idiot!' said Joanna fondly. 'You still can't believe your luck, can you? Why do you think Darroch flaked out? He's never going to let you get away from here any more than Matt would let me go. I know exactly how you're feeling—I'll tell you my story some time.'

'I won't be here. I'll be torn to shreds and packed up and sent away. It's wishful thinking, Jo. Happily married people are always like this, wanting to tie up other people. How can I stay?'

'Why not? Darroch must be mighty relieved to find out you aren't Becky, seeing he's been fighting what he thought was an unlawful attraction for his cousin's fiancée for weeks. Becky's gone for good, so what's the matter with you?'

Rebecca gazed at her numbly. 'You still can't see? *You've* never known what it is to look so like someone else it robs you of your own individuality. But added to all that, at the most momentous time of my whole life, it's a complete barrier to my staying here even if

Darroch could forgive me, even if he asked me to stay. I'll repeat what I said when you rescued me. Didn't you take it in? I'm the living image of Lennox's first love. How *can* I stay? You and Matt didn't answer when I said that. So even if it didn't register with you, Matt knows I couldn't.'

Joanna started to say something, but checked herself. Then she said, 'Rebecca, that can be overcome, I'm sure. Now don't ask me why I feel that way, just let me get you all dolled up. Those men'll burst in if I don't hurry!'

'Then let me go as I am. I don't want to be dolled up. That's what Becky would do—use her looks. But I don't care.'

'Well, I do. So stand still. What a good job your hair dries so quickly. But you're not to leave it loose. That's Becky's style, not yours. I like it drawn back.'

Rebecca said, 'Stop it! Give me my jeans. Perhaps I *should* look as like Becky as I can, though, then they'll know I can't stay here. Besides, finding out what a rotten little liar I am, all Darroch's fondness for me will have disappeared like snow in summer. It was probably nothing but being cooped up here together, anyway—Joanna, not a dress. I'm not dressing up. You don't need to for an exit line.'

But Joanna had the one case Rebecca had left in her wardrobe open and was dragging out a blue dress with a faint green pattern all over it. It had a swathed chiffon scarf cowled softly about the neckline. The chiffon was neither blue nor green nor turquoise but a blend of all, like Rebecca Menteith's eyes. Joanna had her into it in a couple of shakes. Joanna was spilling things out of the case in her eagerness. 'Ah, here's a ribbon. Peacock blue—ideal!' She gave one of her expert twirls with a brush she'd snatched from Nan's room, and tied Rebecca's hair firmly back, high on her head. Then she said in a disappointed tone, 'I suppose your eye-shadow is at the bottom of the river. Has Sylvie left any in this bathroom?'

Rebecca's tone brooked no opposition. 'I will not, under any circumstances, wear eye-shadow. This isn't a stage-show.'

They heard Matt's voice bawling from the end of the passage, 'Girls, come on, Darroch's beside himself— to say nothing of me!'

'I'm coming,' said Rebecca, and went quickly past Joanna, past Matt, straight into the lounge. She was glad it wasn't the kitchen where the men and children could burst in on their return. When you were on the carpet you didn't want too many witnesses.

She was most surprised when Matt and Joanna scuttled in after her. But what did it matter, seeing Meg was already there, sitting in one of the big chairs? Some-one had put a match to the fire, but Rebecca didn't feel cold. She felt burning. Burning with shame and humilia-tion.

Darroch, still in his old cords and huge oatmeal sweater, was standing in front of the fire, very much in charge, arms folded, lips pressed together.

Rebecca burst out, '*I* didn't want to dress up—Jo made me. I want you to get Gwill in to fly me out, to-morrow at the latest. Doesn't matter who knows now.'

Darroch said, 'Don't be stupid, Rebecca. And sit down, you've had a big ordeal.'

She set her chin. 'I won't sit down! I'll stand. I'll take whatever tongue-bashing you like to give me. It will be nothing to the way I've mentally tongue-bashed myself. But just get it over and done with.'

Darroch said, 'Right, but the audience can remove themselves.' He looked expectantly from one to the other of the three. Not one of them moved an inch. Meg said sturdily, 'Never in your life. I don't know what you're aiming to say, Darroch, but as for me, I could kiss Rebecca's feet for taking Becky's place. I came here breathing fire and vengeance and found my fears were all unfounded. You're a bigger fool than I took you for, Darroch Fordyce, if you let her get away from Craigievar.'

'And you're a bigger if you think she's got a chance, Meg King. The only reason I want you all out of it is that naturally I don't want any witnesses to my formal proposal of marriage to Rebecca Menteith. No man would.'

Matt said: 'Good grief . . . no man, I know, would, but that's exactly what *I* got. My dear elderly cousin was present at mine, so why should you fare any better? I'm not here on your behalf, man. I don't want to spoil anything for you, certainly, but in fact I'm sticking around to see Rebecca gets a square deal. I'd also like to persuade her to have you, because she's got some bee in her bonnet that all that's happened makes it impossible for her to marry you. Now, don't interrupt, Joanna, I'm doing fine.'

Rebecca was standing like a graven image. Could she be hearing right? But even if he wanted to marry her, there was still Lennox. All very well for Meg to be so generous, but how would Lennox feel? About returning here if she was there?

Joanna said, her eyes very bright, her ginger cowlick standing up like a rooster's comb, 'Darroch, get on with it, please! Matt doesn't know, but Meg whispered it to me while Rebecca was in the bath. You see, the bee she has in her bonnet is that she can't marry you because she'd remind Lennox morning, noon and night of his late lamented infatuation. So, Darroch Fordyce, it's over to you. And don't ask us to go, because we *won't.*'

He faced her from the hearthrug. 'Listen, Rebecca, and take it in. Aunt Davina met up with Lennox in Fiji—her cruise ship called there. You know he's always loved ships and the sea and messing about with boats? Just one stage better than he loves the mountains. There was a guest-house up for sale in Fiji. A fleet, practically, of small pleasure launches goes with it. Aunt Davina left the cruise. The money she would have put into land here for Lennox can go into this. It would be a paradise for him. For Len and Meg. I was in such a quandary. I loved you—thinking you were Becky—and didn't know how I could do this to him. To you. I thought you'd come back for his sake. I didn't know he'd had the sense to know his future lay with Meg.'

Rebecca just didn't believe it. She closed her eyes, swayed a little, then opened them and looked at Meg. 'And you, Meg? Won't you miss your mountains?'

'I'll be with Lennox,' said Meg. It was enough.

Darroch's eyes lit up. He made a gesture towards the door. 'Out, you three,' he said.

Matt stood his ground. 'The formal proposal first,' he said, eyes alight with mischief.

Darroch groaned, 'What man needs enemies when he has friends like these? I yield. Rebecca Menteith, will you marry me?'

They all gazed at her, not only Darroch. Life was flowing back into her. Her smile began slowly, widened. She had starry lights in the blue-green eyes. '*You bet your sweet life I will*,' she said.

The spectators collapsed into laughter. 'What prosaic language for a writer,' mourned Joanna. 'All right, we'll go, Darroch. The rest will be said much more romantically, but not in words.'

So suddenly, blessedly, they were alone. Darroch, for so big a man, was always a fast mover, but never had he achieved a speed like this. Rebecca put out her hands, but they were never taken. She was engulfed, hungrily, passionately ... crushed against him. Darroch said, 'No more feelings of guilt, no more bewilderment. Darling, sweetheart, you're mine. You're real. You're not Becky.

You're not Len's ex-fiancée. You're Rebecca!'

Thereafter speech was neither necessary nor possible.

They had half an hour. At the end of that time Joanna tapped to say she could hear the truck returning with the men and the children. They looked at each other aghast, then Rebecca put her hand to her mouth. 'What can we tell them? The children specially?'

Darroch said, 'My love, I'm going to tell them the truth. There's nothing else for it. Children are wonderful. They can't bear secrecy and mystery, the things grown-ups try to keep from them. They'll just accept it as part of the weird and wonderful things that adults do. But we'll do it my way. Come and sit over here, by the fire, as if you were a visitor. Not in the kitchen buttering pikelets for them as usual. Now wait here.'

He went through to the back porch where the men and the children were kicking off gumboots. He said to them, 'Don't bother cleaning up. We want you to come through to the lounge, we have a surprise for you.'

'I love surprises,' said Nan. 'Is it a nice one?'

'A very nice one. You'll certainly love this. It's a visitor.'

They played a guessing game as they followed him. Was it Aunt Fan? Was it Gran and Granddad? It couldn't be Mummy back because she wasn't a visitor and Meg, as she opened the door, said it wasn't her. They ran in, stopped, peered round for the visitor, saw Becky, as they thought, sitting in an armchair in a pretty dress they'd never seen before. The men had halted in their tracks and looked all round too.

Darroch, grinning hugely, stepped across to the armchair, put a hand on Rebecca's shoulder, said, 'This isn't Becky, children, chaps. It's her cousin Rebecca.'

Six pairs of staring eyes resulted. Lindsay said, not pausing to greet a stranger, because she didn't even look strange, 'How did *she* get here? We did see the Heronscrag hacks in the paddock. What's going on? And what are you looking so chipper about, Darroch?'

Darroch's warm brown eyes danced. 'I'm looking chipper because I've just got engaged. I'm going to marry Rebecca.'

Duncan got such a shock he sat down on the arm of Joanna's chair. 'I have a feeling I'm going mad. Aye, that's it. I've thocht for a wee while I might be. I've had some very strange conversations with Becky of late. I felt either she was losing her memory, or I was. Now this. And where *is* the other lass?—Becky?'

Andrew said, 'Yes, where's Becky? I want to show her my snail.'

Darroch said, 'You can show her in a minute, Andrew.'

Keith scratched his red head. 'I don't get it. There's something funny about this. That T.V. programme we saw down at the quarters—Becky's cousin Rebecca was on a cruise ship. She ought to be somewhere in the middle of the Pacific, yet here she is, large as life, as like Becky as two peas in a pod, and you say she's engaged to you. But you'd never met her. I've known some speedy workers in my time, but this beats all!'

'*I want to show Becky my snail!*' said Andrew on a louder note.

Darroch bent down, took his hand, led him to the hearth and said, 'Here she is. It's a bit hard to understand, but the first Becky who was going to marry Uncle Lennox ran away and her cousin Rebecca, who is exactly like her, came up here to try to put things right, and I thought she was Becky. So she decided to play a trick on us. Remember how Becky told you they often mixed people up when they were little? Played pranks on them. She found she was needed to look after us, thought we'd be cross with Becky for running away, so pretended she was Becky. Wasn't it naughty of her?'

'No,' said Andrew simply. It just didn't matter to him. He looked up into Rebecca's face, smiled his slow smile, laid his offering in her lap, said, 'It's the best snail I've ever found. It's a beauty, and not a bit squashed. You can have him, Becky. What'll you call him?'

Rebecca didn't bat an eyelash. 'My very first engagement present,' she said. 'Thank you, Andrew. Meg, would you get a cabbage leaf out of the vegie rack? I'll call him Sylvester. He makes a silver trail.'

Duncan was recovering. 'It's come to me,' he said, 'that that Becky's the one on the cruise ship. I never knew such a change. It had me fair puzzled. But how's young Lennox going to take this?'

Rebecca looked up from stroking the snail. 'Darroch, you must tell them about the guest-house and the launches ... and that Lennox is going to marry Meg.'

Their delight in this last piece of news was heart-warming to see. Meg blushed rosily. It made Rebecca think of something. 'Darroch, I know you thought I was Becky, but why in the world, after your Aunt Davy rang you, didn't you tell me Len wasn't coming back to Craigievar?'

'Because I didn't know then he was going to marry Meg. I thought you were Becky and might very well fancy a glamorous existence on a tropical isle, much more than Craigievar. Even against all my better judgement, I couldn't let you go.'

Duncan heaved himself out of the chair he'd dropped into. 'I'm going to start kissing all these brides right now,' he said, seizing Meg. 'Come on, chaps ... and if we don't get a champagne dinner out of a double engagement, we ought to, at that!'

His words had a strange effect on the three women. They looked horrified. Then Joanna found her voice. 'Tell me, Rebecca, before all the hoo-ha started, what *had* you intended to have for dinner tonight? Could you, by any stroke of good luck, have thawed out a Canada goose or some venison?'

Rebecca shook her head. 'Not as much as some chops.

I took out two pounds of plain old beef mince at lunch-time.' She started to giggle. 'Mince and champagne sound fine to me.'

Joanna said, 'Well, even if I was once the most igno-rant cook in all the Mackenzie country, I do know ways of serving up mince. It can be mince balls with bacon and pineapple rings. Meg, men, children, into the kitchen to help.'

'No fear,' said Nan. 'I've loads of questions to ask Becky—Rebecca. Who do you want for a bridesmaid, Rebecca?'

'Well, certainly not my cousin,' she said, laughing. 'Who do you think, Nan? What colour do you fancy, love?'

Darroch groaned. 'I've a feeling that from now on we men will be superfluous! But before I go and take the poor males out with me, I'm saying one thing about my wedding. No talk about waiting till after Christmas. It's to be next month, before lambing. I don't intend to wait. And we'll have it down here in the little church among the mountains. Your parents won't mind, Rebecca?'

'No, we'll let them know tonight. They'll be so relieved to know I've confessed at last. They'll probably fly down right away.'

Darroch was laughing, 'And if the Rubicon floods be-fore the wedding-day, we'll get them to lift us out by helicopter. Now, come on, I can hardly wait to get this sumptuous engagement feast ready!'

It was midnight before Darroch and Rebecca said good-night. As the others tactfully retired, he said, 'I've a whim to see you to your door. Remember that other night? But tonight I needn't feel guilty about snatching a kiss from my cousin's fiancée. Proxy indeed ... it was just that I couldn't resist it.'

They came to her door. There was no moon tonight, but a brilliancy of stars shone through the little window at the end of the passage.

'I love this view,' whispered Rebecca. 'It was tearing my heart out to leave it. Now I never will.'

'I hope there's one view you'll love even more, love.'

'Which?'

'The view from my window. When you move in with me. It looks down on the Rubicon, remember?'

'Dear Rubicon,' said Rebecca, her lips against his chin.

Darroch's voice was horrified. '*Dear* Rubicon, when it so nearly took you from me? I'll relive that moment for years in nightmares!'

'No, my darling. The Rubicon will be the river that encircles our own little world.' She sighed, leaning against him dreamily. 'Oh, Darroch, that other night! I was so miserable. I envied Joanna and Verona so.'

He pulled her closer. 'Why? Tell me why?'

She laughed. 'I'll tell you another time. When I don't need to envy them any more. Darroch, we won't have to be away too long on our honeymoon, will we? Because best of all will be coming back here.'

He said, rather thickly, 'I'll have to go. Suddenly even an October wedding seems too far away. I'll be good, as I was that night.' He brushed his lips over hers, as he had done in that first kiss when he had thought she was Becky. And he was gone.

Five weeks later, and they were home. They had been married eight days, but this was the first night they would ever spend together among their beloved mountains.

Sylvie and Ewan and the children had prepared a wonderful welcome home dinner for them, but now they were across at Kildrummy and not even their lights could be seen. It had been hilarious. The river was up, so Gwillym had flown them in.

They gazed out of the window that looked on to

Craigievar Crag, they could hear the waters rushing along. There had been fresh snow on the peaks, and in the light of another full moon, it looked like a scene from Switzerland.

Darroch was teasing Rebecca. 'Imagine coming home from a honeymoon on a tropical island like Norfolk Island to this ... you must be crazy, Mrs Fordyce.'

'This is our true world, Darroch. All I'll ever want. Darroch, I once stood here swept with longings. Longings I thought would never be realised. All bound up with you, and not wanting to leave here, and all hopeless.'

She could tell by his voice he was smiling. 'And you were envious of Joanna and Verona. Going to tell me why?'

She said simply, 'Because they'd had a romantic evening but didn't have to say goodnight. Because you'd just left me. Because they lay beside the ones they loved. There are other heights beside the mountain heights, Darroch. As we know now.'

'As we know so well now,' he said, and led her along to his room.

4 FREE
Harlequin Romances

Get all the latest books before they're sold out!

As a Harlequin subscriber you actually receive your personal copies of the latest Romances immediately after they come off the press, so you're sure of getting all 6 each month.

Cancel your subscription whenever you wish!

You don't have to buy any minimum number of books. Whenever you decide to stop your subscription just let us know and we'll cancel all further shipments.

Your FREE gift includes

- **Anne Hampson** — Beyond the Sweet Waters
- **Anne Mather** — The Arrogant Duke
- **Violet Winspear** — Cap Flamingo
- **Nerina Hilliard** — Teachers Must Learn

FREE GIFT CERTIFICATE

and Subscription Reservation

Mail this coupon today!

In U.S.A.:
Harlequin Reader Service
MPO Box 707
Niagara Falls, NY 14302

In Canada:
Harlequin Reader Service
649 Ontario Street
Stratford, Ontario
N5A 6W4

Harlequin Reader Service:

Please send me my 4 Harlequin Romance novels
FREE. Also, reserve a subscription to the 6 NEW
Harlequin Romance novels published each month.
Each month I will receive 6 NEW Romance novels at
the low price of $1.25 each (Total — $7.50 a month).
There are no shipping and handling or any other
hidden charges. I may cancel this arrangement at any
time, but even if I do, these first 4 books are still mine
to keep.

_____

NAME   (PLEASE PRINT)

_____

ADDRESS

_____

CITY   STATE/PROV.   ZIP/POSTAL CODE

Offer not valid to present subscribers
Offer expires June 30, 1980   00356436100

What readers say about Harlequin Romances

"I can't imagine my reading life without Harlequin."

J.L.,* Sioux Falls, South Dakota

"I just read my first three Harlequins. It is Sunday today, otherwise I would go back to the bookstore to get some more."

E.S., Kingston, Ontario

"I'm really hooked and I love it."

M.S., Richmond, Virginia

"Harlequins help me to escape from housework into a world of romance, adventure and travel."

J.R., Glastonbury, Connecticut

*Names available on request

What readers say about Harlequin Romances

"Harlequins take away the world's troubles and for a while you can live in a world of your own where love reigns supreme."
L.S.,* Beltsville, Maryland

"Thank you for bringing romance back to me."
J.W., Tehachapi, California

"I find Harlequins are the only stories on the market that give me a satisfying romance with sufficient depth without being maudlin."
C.S., Bangor, Maine

"Harlequins are magic carpets...away from pain and depression...away to other people and other countries one might never know otherwise."
H.R., Akron, Ohio

*Names available on request